"Are you sure we should be doing this?"

There was a slight easing of the tension around his mouth. "We're not robbing a bank, Violet."

"I know, but—"

"If you'd rather not, then I can always find someone—"

"No," Violet said, not even wanting to think about the someone else he would take. "I'll go. It'll be fun—I haven't been out to dinner for ages."

He smiled a lopsided smile that made the back of Violet's knees feel weak. "There's one other thing..."

You want it to be a real date? You want us to see each other as in "see each other"? You've secretly been in love with me for years and years and years? Violet forced herself to keep her expression blank while the thoughts pushed against the door of her reasoning like people trying to get into a closeout sale.

"We'll have to act like a normal dating couple," he said. "Hold hands, show affection...and so on."

And so on?

What else did he mean?

Violet nodded like her head was supported by an elastic band instead of neck muscles. "Fine. Of course. Good idea. Fab. Brilliant idea. We have to look authentic. Wouldn't want anyone to get the wrong idea... I mean, well, you know what I mean."

Cam leaned down and brushed her cheek with his lips, the slight graze of his rougher skin making something in her stomach turn over. "I'll pick you up at seven."

Melanie Milburne read her first Harlequin at age seventeen in between studying for her final exams. After completing a master's degree in education, she decided to write a novel in between settling down to do a PhD. She became so hooked on writing romance, the PhD was shelved and her career as a romance writer was born. Melanie is an ambassador for the Australian Childhood Foundation and is a keen dog lover and trainer and enjoys long walks in the Tasmanian bush.

Books by Melanie Milburne

Harlequin Presents

His Mistress for a Week
At No Man's Command
His Final Bargain
Uncovering the Silveri Secret

The Ravensdale Scandals

The Most Scandalous Ravensdale
Ravensdale's Defiant Captive
Awakening the Ravensdale Heiress
Engaged to Her Ravensdale Enemy

The Chatsfield

Chatsfield's Ultimate Acquisition

The Playboys of Argentina

The Valquez Bride
The Valquez Seduction

Those Scandalous Caffarellis

Never Say No to a Caffarelli
Never Underestimate a Caffarelli
Never Gamble with a Caffarelli

Visit the Author Profile page at Harlequin.com for more titles.

Melanie Milburne

UNWRAPPING HIS CONVENIENT FIANCÉE

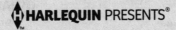

ISBN-13: 978-0-373-13486-1

Unwrapping His Convenient Fiancée

First North American Publication 2016

Copyright © 2016 by Melanie Milburne

Printed in U.S.A.

www.Harlequin.com

UNWRAPPING HIS
CONVENIENT FIANCÉE

To my dear friend Jo Shearing. You are such a gorgeous person and I value our friendship so much. This one is for you. xxxx

CHAPTER ONE

IT WAS THE invitation Violet had been dreading for months. Ten years in a row she had gone to the office Christmas party *sans* partner. *Ten years!* Every year she told herself next year would be different, and yet here she was staring at the red and silver invitation with her stomach in a sinkhole of despair *again*. It was bad enough fielding the *What, no date?* looks and comments from her female colleagues. But it was the thought of being in a crowded room that was the real torture. With all those jostling bodies pressing up so close she wouldn't be able to breathe.

Male bodies.

Bodies that were much bigger and stronger and more powerful than hers—especially when they were drunk...

Violet blinked away the memory. She hardly ever thought about *that* party these days. Well, only now and again. She had come to a fragile sort of peace over it. The self-blame had eased even if the lingering shame had not.

But she was nearly thirty and it was time to move on. More than time. Which meant going to the Christmas party to prove to herself she was back in control of her life.

However, there was the agony of deciding what to wear. Her accountancy firm's Christmas party was considered one of the premier events in the financial sector's calendar. It wasn't just a drinks and nibbles affair. It was an annual gala with champagne flowing like a fountain and Michelin star quality food and dancing to a live band. Every year there was a theme and everyone was expected to be part of the action to demonstrate their commitment to office harmony. This year's theme was *A Star-Struck Christmas*. Which would mean Violet would have to find something Hollywoodish to wear. She wasn't good at glamour. She didn't like drawing attention to herself. She wasn't good at partying full stop.

Violet slipped the invitation between the pages of her book and sighed. Even the London lunchtime café crowd was rubbing in her singleton status. Everyone was a couple. She was the only person sitting on her own. Even a couple pushing ninety were at the table in the window *and* they were holding hands. That would be her parents in thirty years. Still with the magic buzzing between them as it had from the first moment they'd met. Just like her three siblings with their perfect partners. Building their lives together, having children and doing all the things she dreamed of doing.

Violet had watched each of her siblings fall in love. Fast-living Fraser first, racy Rose next and then laid-back Lily. Been to each of their weddings. Been a bridesmaid three times. *Three times. Groan.* She was always in the audience watching romance develop and blossom, but she longed to be on the stage.

Why couldn't she find someone perfect for her?

Was there something wrong with her? Guys occasionally asked her out but it never went past a date or two. Her natural shyness didn't make for scintillating conversation and she had no idea how to flirt… Well, she did if she had a few drinks but that was a mistake she was *not* going to repeat. The problem was that men were so impatient these days, or maybe they always had been that way. But she was not going to sleep with someone just because it was expected of her…or because she was too drunk to say no. She wanted to feel attracted to a man and to feel his attraction to her. To feel frissons of red-hot desire scoot all over her flesh at his touch. To melt when his gaze met hers. To shiver with delight when he pressed his lips to hers.

Not that too many male lips had been pressed to hers lately. She couldn't remember the last time she had been really kissed by a man. Pecks on the cheek from her father and brother or grandfather didn't count.

Violet was rubbish at the dating game. Rubbish. Rubbish. Rubbish. She was going to end up an old and wrinkled spinster living with a hundred and fifty-two cats. With a chest of drawers full of exquisitely embroidered baby clothes for the babies she had longed for since she was a little girl.

'Is this seat taken?'

Violet glanced up at the familiar deep baritone voice, a faint shiver coursing down her spine when her gaze connected with her older brother's best friend from university.

'Cam?' Her voice came out like the sound of a squeaky toy, an annoying habit she hadn't been able to correct since first meeting Cameron McKinnon. She had been eighteen when her brother brought Cam home for the summer—or at least the Scottish version of it—to their family's estate, Drummond Brae, in the Highlands. 'What are you doing here? How are you? Fraser told me you've been living in

Greece designing a yacht for someone super-rich. How's it all going? When did you get back?'

Shut up! Funny, but she was never lost for words around Cam. She talked *too* much. She couldn't seem to help it nor could she explain it. He wasn't intimidating or threatening in any way. He was polite, if a little aloof, but he had been a part of her family for long enough for her to get over herself.

But clearly she *hadn't* got over herself.

Cam pulled out the chair opposite and sat down, his knees gently bumping against Violet's underneath the table. The touch was like an electric current moving through her body, heating her in places that had no business being heated. Not by her brother's best friend. Cam was out of her league. Way out.

'I was in the area for a meeting. It finished early and I remembered you mentioning this café once so thought I'd check it out,' he said. 'I've only been back a couple of days. My father is getting remarried just before Christmas.'

Violet's eyes widened to the size of the saucer under her skinny latte. 'Again? How many times is that now? Three? Four?'

His mouth twisted. 'Five. And there's another baby on the way, which brings the total of half-siblings to six, plus the seven step-siblings, so eleven all together.'

Violet thought her three nephews, two nieces and the baby in the making were a handful—she couldn't imagine eleven. 'How on earth do you keep track of all of their birthdays?'

His half smile looked a little weary around the edges. 'I've set up automatic transfers via online banking. Takes the guesswork out.'

'Maybe I should do that.' Violet stirred her coffee for something to do with her hands. Being in Cam's company—not that it happened much these days—always made her feel like a gauche schoolgirl in front of a college professor. He was an unusual counterpoint to her older brother who was a laugh a minute, life of the party type. Cam was more serious in nature with a tendency to frown rather than smile.

Her gaze drifted towards his mouth—another habit she couldn't quite control when she was around him. His lips were fairly evenly sculpted, although the lower one had a slightly more sensual fullness to it that made her think of long, blood-heating, pulse-racing kisses.

Not that Violet had ever kissed him. Men like Cameron McKinnon didn't kiss girls like her. She was too girl-next-door. He dated women who looked as if they had just stepped out of a photo shoot. Glamorous, sophisticated types who could hold their own in any company without breaking out in hives in case someone spoke to them.

Cam's gaze briefly went to her bare left hand where she was cradling her coffee before coming back to hers in a keenly focused look that made something deep in her belly unfurl like a flower opening its petals to the sun.

'So, how are things with you, Violet?'

'Erm…okay.' At least she wasn't breaking out into hives, but the blush she could feel crawling over her cheeks was almost as bad. Was he thinking—like the rest of her family—*Three times a bridesmaid, never a bride*?

'Only okay?' His look had a serious note to it, a combination of concern and concentration, as if she were the only person he wanted to talk to right then. It was one of the things Violet liked about him—one of the many things. He wasn't so full of himself that he couldn't spare the time to listen. She often wondered if he'd been around to talk to after that wretched party, during her first and only year at university, her life might not have turned out the way it had.

Violet stretched her mouth into her standard everything-is-cool-with-me smile. 'I'm fine. Just busy with work and Christmas shopping and stuff. Like you, I have a lot of people to buy for now with all my nephews and nieces. Did you know Lily and Cooper are expecting? Mum and Dad are planning the usual big Christmas at Drummond Brae. Has Mum invited you? She said she was going to. The doctors think it will be Grandad's last Christmas so we're all making an effort to be there for him.'

Cam's mouth took on a rueful slant. 'My father's decided to upstage Christmas with his wedding on Christmas Eve.'

'Where's it being held?'

'Here in London.'

'Maybe you could fly up afterwards,' Violet said. 'Or have you got other commitments?' Other commitments such as a girlfriend. Surely he would have one. Men like Cam wouldn't go long between lovers. He was too handsome, too rich, too intelligent, too sexy. Too everything. Cam had never broadcast his relationships with women the way her brother Fraser had before he'd fallen madly in love with Zoe. Cam was intensely private about his private life. So private it made Violet wonder if he had a secret lover stashed away somewhere, someone he kept out of the glaring spotlight that his work as an internationally acclaimed naval architect attracted.

'I'll see,' he said. 'Mum will expect a visit, especially now that her third husband Hugh's left her.'

Violet frowned. 'Oh, no. I'm sorry to hear that. Is she terribly upset?'

Cam gave her a speaking look. 'Not particularly. He drank. A lot.'

'Oh…'

Cam's family history was nothing short of a saga. Not that he'd ever said much about it to her, but Fraser had filled in the gaps. His parents went through a bitter divorce when he was six and promptly remarried and set up new families, collecting other biological children and stepchildren along the way. Cam was jostled between the various households until he was sent to boarding school when he was eight. Violet could picture him as a little boy—studious, quietly observing on the sidelines, not making a fuss and avoiding one where it was made. He was still like that. When he came to visit her family for weddings, christenings or other gatherings he was always on the fringe, standing back with a drink in his hand he rarely touched, quietly measuring the scene with his navy-blue gaze.

The waitress came over to take Cam's order with a smile that went beyond *I'm your server, can I help you?* to *Do you want my number?*

Violet tried to ignore the little dart of jealousy

that spiked her in the gut. It was none of her business who he flirted with. Why should she care if he picked up a date from her favourite café? Even if she had been coming here for years and no one had asked for *her* number.

Cam looked across the table at her. 'Would you like another coffee?'

Violet put her hand over the top of her latte glass. 'No, I'm good.'

'Just a long black, thanks,' Cam said to the waitress with a brief but polite smile.

Violet waited until the girl had left before she spoke. 'Cra—ack.'

His brow furrowed. 'Pardon?'

She gave him a teasing smile. 'Didn't you hear that girl's heart breaking?'

He looked puzzled for a moment, and then faintly annoyed. 'She's not my type.'

'Describe your type.' *Why had she asked that?*

The bridge between Cam's ink-black eyebrows was still pleated in three tight vertical lines. 'I've been too busy for any type just lately.' His phone, which was sitting on the table, beeped with a message and he glanced at it before turning off the screen, his lips pressing so firmly his mouth turned bone-white.

'What's wrong?'

He forcibly relaxed his features. 'Nothing.'

The phone beeped again and his mouth flattened once more. He clicked the mute button and slipped the phone into his jacket pocket as the waitress set his coffee down on the table between them. 'So, how's work?'

Violet glanced at the invitation peeping out of the pages of her book. Was it her imagination or was it flashing like a beacon? She surreptitiously pushed it back out of sight. 'Fine…'

Cam followed the line of her gaze. 'What's that?'

'Nothing… Just an invitation.'

'To?'

Violet was sure her cheeks were as the red as the baubles on the invitation. 'The office Christmas party.'

'You going?'

She couldn't meet his gaze and looked at the sugar bowl instead. Who knew there were so many different artificial sweeteners these days? Amazing. 'I kind of have to… It's expected in the interests of office harmony.'

'You don't sound too keen.'

Violet lifted one of her shoulders in a shrug. 'Yeah, well, I'm not really a party girl.' Not any more. Her first and only attempt at partying had ended in a blurry haze of regret and self-recrimination. An event she was still, all these years on, trying to put behind her with varying degrees of success.

But secret shame cast a long shadow.

'It's a pretty big affair, isn't it?' Cam said. 'No expense spared and so on, I take it?'

Violet rolled her eyes. 'Ironic when you consider it's a firm of bean counters.'

'Pretty successful bean counters,' Cam said. 'Well done you for nailing a job there.'

Violet didn't like to admit how far from her dream job it actually was. After quitting her university studies, a clerical job in a large accounting firm had seemed a good place to blend into the background. But what had suited her at nineteen was feeling less satisfying as she approached thirty. She couldn't shake off the nagging feeling she should be doing more with her life. Extending herself. Reaching her potential instead of placing limitations on herself. But since that party... Well, everything had been put on pause. It was like her life had jammed and she couldn't move forward.

The vibration of Cam's phone drew Violet's gaze to his top pocket. Not just to his top pocket but his chest in general. He was built like an endurance athlete, tall and lean with muscles where a man needed them to be and where a woman most liked to see them. And she was no exception. His skin was tanned and his dark brown hair had some surface highlights where the strong sunlight of Greece had caught and lightened it. He had cleanly shaven skin, but there was enough dark stubble to suggest he hadn't been holding the door for everyone else when the testosterone was dished out.

'Aren't you going to answer that?' Violet asked.

'It'll keep.'

'Work or family?'

'Neither.'

Violet's eyebrows lifted along with her intrigue. 'A woman?'

He took out the phone and held his finger on the off switch with a determined set to his features. 'Yeah. One that won't take no for an answer.'

'How long have you been dating her?'

'I haven't been dating her.' Cam's expression was grim. 'She's a client's wife. A valuable client.'

'Oh... Tricky.'

'Very. To the tune of about forty million pounds tricky.'

Forty million? Violet came from a wealthy background but even she had trouble getting her head around a figure like that. Cam designed yachts for the super-wealthy. He'd won a heap of awards for his designs and become extremely wealthy in the process. Some of the yachts he designed were massive, complete with marble en suite bathrooms with hot tubs, and dining and sitting rooms that were plush and palatial. One yacht even had its own library and lap swimming pool. But, even so, it amazed her how much a rich person would pay for a yacht they only used now and again. 'Seriously? You're being paid forty million to design a yacht?'

'No, that's the cost of the yacht once it's complete,' he said. 'But I get paid a pretty decent amount to design it.'

How much was *pretty decent*? Violet longed to ask but decided against it out of politeness. 'So… what will you do? Keep ignoring this woman's calls and messages?'

He let out a short, gusty breath. 'I'll have to get the message across one way or the other. I'm not the sort of guy who gets mixed up with married women.' His mouth twisted again. 'That would be my father.'

'Maybe if she sees you've got someone else it will drive home the message.' Violet picked up her almost empty latte and looked at him over the rim of the glass. '*Is* there someone else?' *Arrgh! Why did you ask that?*

Cam's gaze met hers and that warm sensation bloomed deep and low in her belly again. His dark blue eyes were fringed with thick ink-black lashes she would have killed for. There was something about his intelligent eyes that always made her feel he saw more than he let on. 'No,' he said. 'You?'

Violet coughed out a self-effacing laugh. 'Don't *you* start. I get enough of that from my family, not to mention my friends and flatmates.'

Cam gave her a wry smile. 'I don't know what's wrong with the young men of London. You should've been snapped up long ago.'

A pin drop silence fell between them.

Violet looked at her coffee glass as if it were the most fascinating thing she had ever seen. The way her cheeks were going, the café's chef would be coming out to cook the toast on her face to save on electricity. How had she got into this conversation? Awkward. Awkward. Awkward. How long was the canyon of silence going to last? Should she say something?

But what?

Her mind was blank.

She was hopeless at small talk. It was another reason she was terrible at parties. The idle conversation gene had skipped her. Her sisters and brother were the ones who could talk their way out of or into any situation. She was the wallflower of the family. All those years of being overshadowed by

verbose older siblings and super articulate parents
had made her conversationally challenged. She was
used to standing back and letting others do the talking. Even her tendency to gabble like a fool around
Cam had suddenly deserted her.

'When's your office party?'

Violet blinked and refocused her gaze on Cam's.
'Erm…tomorrow.'

'Would you like me to come with you?'

Violet had trouble keeping her jaw off the table
and her heart from skipping right out of her chest
and landing in his lap. *Best not think about his lap.*
'But why would you want to do that?'

He gave a casual shrug of one broad shoulder.
'I'm free tomorrow night. Thought it might help you
mingle if you had a wingman, so to speak.'

Violet gave him a measured look. 'Is this a pity
date?'

'It's not a date, period.' Something about his adamant tone rankled. 'Just a friend helping out a
friend.'

Violet had enough friends. It was a date she
wanted. A proper date. Not with a man on a mercy
mission. Did he think she was completely useless?
A romance tragic who couldn't find a prince to
take her to the ball? She didn't even *want* to go
to the ball, thank you very much. The ball wasn't

that special. All those people drinking and eating too much and dancing till the wee hours to music so loud you couldn't hear yourself shout, let alone think. 'Thanks for the offer but I'll be fine.'

Violet pushed her coffee glass to one side and picked up her book. But, before she could leave the table, Cam's hand came down on her forearm. 'I didn't mean to upset you.'

'I'm not upset.' Violet knew her crisp tone belied her statement. Of course she was upset. Who wouldn't be? He was rescuing her. What could be more insulting than a man asking you out because he felt sorry for you? Had Fraser said something to him? Had one of her sisters? Her parents? Her grandfather? Why couldn't everyone mind their own business? All she got these days was pressure. *Why aren't you dating anyone? You're too fussy. You're almost thirty.* It never ended.

The warmth of Cam's broad hand seeped through the layers of her winter clothing, awakening her flesh like a heat pack on a frostbitten limb. 'Hey.'

Violet hadn't pouted since she was about five but she pouted now. She could find a date. Sure she could. She could sign up to one of any number of dating websites or apps and have a hundred dates. If she put her mind to it she could be engaged by

Christmas. Well, maybe that was pushing it a bit. 'I'm perfectly able to find my own date, okay?'

He gave her arm the tiniest squeeze before releasing it. 'Of course.' He sat back in his chair, his forehead creased in a slight frown. 'I'm sorry. It was a bad idea. Seriously bad.'

Why was it? And why *seriously* bad? Violet cradled her book close to her chest where her heart was beating a little too fast. Not fast enough to call for a defibrillator but not far off. His touch had done something to her, like he had turned a setting on in her body she hadn't known she'd had. Her senses were sitting up and alert instead of slumped and listless. Had he ever touched her before? She tried to think… Sometimes in the past he would kiss her on the cheek, a chaste brotherly sort of kiss. But lately…since Easter, in fact…there had been no physical contact from him. None at all. It was as if he had deliberately kept his distance. That last holiday weekend at home, she remembered him coming into one of the sitting rooms at Drummond Brae and going straight back out again with a muttered apology when he'd found her curled up on one of the sofas with her embroidery. Why had he done that? What was wrong with her that he couldn't bear to be left alone with her?

Violet picked up her scarf and wound it around her neck. 'I have to get back to work. I hope your father's wedding goes well.'

'It should do, he's had enough practice.' He drained his coffee and stood, snatching his jacket from the back of the chair and slinging it over his shoulder. 'I'll walk you back to your office. I'm heading that way.'

Violet knew the tussle over who paid for the coffee was inevitable so when he offered she let him take care of it for once. 'Thanks,' she said once he'd settled the bill.

'No problem.'

He put a gentle hand in the small of her back to guide her out of the way of a young mother coming in with a pram and a squirming, red-faced toddler. The sizzling heat of his touch moved along the entire length of Violet's spine, making her aware of her femininity as if he had stroked her intimately.

Get a grip already.

This was the problem with being desperate and dateless. The slightest brush of a male hand turned her into a wanton fool. Stirring up needs that she hadn't even registered as needs until now.

But it wasn't just any male hand.

It was Cam's hand…connected to a body that

made her think of smoking-hot sex. Not that she knew what smoking-hot sex actually felt like. The only sex she'd had was a surrealist blur with an occasional flashback of two or three male faces looming over her, talking about her, not to her. Definitely not the sort of romantic scene she had envisaged when she'd hit puberty. It was another thing she'd miserably failed at doing. Each of her siblings had successfully navigated their way through the dating minefield, all of them now partnered with their soul mate. *Was* she too fussy? Had that night at that party permanently damaged her self-esteem and sexual confidence? Why should it when she could barely remember it in any detail?

She had been surrounded by love and acceptance all her life. There should be no reason for her to feel inadequate or not quite up to the mark. But somehow love—even a vague liking for someone of the opposite sex—had so far escaped her.

Violet walked out to the footpath with Cam, where the rain had started to fall in icy droplets. She popped open her umbrella but Cam had to bend almost double to gain any benefit from it. He took the handle from her and held the umbrella over both of their heads. Her fingers tingled where his brushed hers, the sensation travelling all through her body as if running along an electric network.

Trying to keep dry, as well as out of the way of the bustling Christmas shopping crowd, put Violet so close to the tall frame of his body she could smell the clean sharp fragrance of his aftershave, the woodsy base notes reminding her of a cool, shaded pine forest. To anyone looking in from the outside they would look like a romantically involved couple, huddled under the same umbrella, Cam's stride considerably slowing to match hers.

They came to the large Victorian building where the accounting firm Violet worked as an accounts clerk was situated. But just as she was about to turn and say her goodbyes to Cam, one of the women who worked with her came click-clacking down the steps. Lorna ran her gaze over Cam's tall figure standing next to Violet. 'Well, well, well. Things finally looking up for you, are they, Violet?'

Violet ground her teeth so hard she could have moonlighted as a nutcracker. Lorna wasn't her favourite workmate, far from it. She had a tendency to gossip to stir up trouble. Violet knew for a fact their boss only kept Lorna on because she was brilliant at her job—and because she was having a full-on affair with him. 'Off to lunch?' she asked, refusing to respond to Lorna's taunt.

Lorna gave an orthodontist's website smile and

aimed her lash-fluttering gaze at Cam. 'Will we be seeing you at the office Christmas party?'

Cam's arm snaked around Violet's waist, a protective band of steel that made every nerve in her body jump up and down and squeal with delight. 'We'll be there.'

We will? Violet waited until Lorna had gone before looking up at Cam's unreadable expression. 'Why on earth did you say that? I told you I didn't want a—'

He stepped out from under the umbrella and placed the handle back in her hand. Violet had to extend her arm upwards to its fullest range to keep the umbrella high enough to maintain eye contact. 'I'll strike a deal with you,' he said. 'I'll come to your Christmas party if you'll come to a dinner with my client tonight.'

Violet screwed up her face. 'The one with the persistent wife?'

'I've been thinking about what you said back at the café. What better way to send her the message I'm not interested than to show her I'm seeing someone?'

'But we're not...' she disguised a little gulp '...*seeing* each other.'

'No, but no one else needs to know that.'

You don't have to be so darned emphatic about

it. Violet chewed at one side of her mouth. 'How are we going to keep this…quiet?'

'You mean from your family?'

'You know what my mother's like.' Violet gave a little eye roll. 'One whiff of us going on a date together, and she'll be posting wedding invitations quicker than you can say *I do.*'

There was another yawning silence.

I do?

Are you nuts? You said the words 'I do' to the man who views weddings like people view the plague!

Something shifted in Cam's expression—a blink of his eyes, a flicker of a muscle in his lean cheek, a stretching of his mouth into a smile that didn't involve his eyes. 'We'll cross that bridge if we come to it.'

If we come to it? There was no *if* about it. That bridge was going to blow up in their faces like a Stage Five firecracker on Guy Fawkes Night. Violet knew her family too well. They were constantly on the lookout for any signs of her dating. MI5 could learn a thing or two from her mother and sisters. How was she going to explain a night out with Cam McKinnon? 'Are you sure we should be doing this?'

There was a slight easing of the tension around his mouth. 'We're not robbing a bank, Violet.'

'I know, but—'

'If you'd rather not, then I can always find some-one—'

'No,' Violet said, not even wanting to think about the 'someone' he would take. 'I'll go. It'll be fun—I haven't been out to dinner for ages.'

He smiled a lopsided smile that made the back of Violet's knees feel like someone was tickling them with a feather. 'There's one other thing...'

You want it to be a real date? You want us to see each other as in 'see each other'? You've se-cretly been in love with me for years and years and years? Violet kept her face blank while the thoughts pushed against the door of her reasoning like people trying to get into a closing down sale.

'We'll have to act like a normal dating couple,' he said. 'Hold hands and...stuff.'

And stuff?

What other stuff?

Violet nodded like her head was supported by an elastic band instead of neck muscles. 'Fine. Of course. Good idea. Fab. Brilliant idea. We have to look authentic. Wouldn't want anyone to get the wrong idea... I mean, well, you know what I mean.'

Cam leaned down and brushed her cheek with his lips, the slight graze of his rougher skin making something in her stomach turn over. 'I'll pick you up at seven.'

Violet took a step backwards to enter the building but stumbled over the first step and would have fallen if it wasn't for Cam's hand shooting out to steady her. 'You okay?' he asked with a concerned frown.

Violet looked at his stubble-surrounded mouth that just moments ago had been against the smooth skin of her cheek. Had he felt that same sensation ricochet through his body? Had he wondered in that infinitesimal moment what it would feel like to press his lips to hers? Not in a brotherly kiss, but a proper man-wants-woman kiss? She sent the point of her tongue over the surface of her lips, her breath hitching when he tracked every millimetre of the movement. *Keep it light.* 'For a moment there I thought you were going to kiss me,' Violet said with a little laugh.

The navy-blue of his gaze turned three shades darker before glancing at her mouth and back again. But then his hand dropped from her arm as if her skin had scorched him. 'Let's not go there.'

But I want *to go there. I want to. I want to. I want to.* Violet kept her smile in place even though it felt like it was stitched to her mouth. 'Yes, that would be taking things too far. I mean, not that I don't find you attractive or anything, but us kissing? Not such a great idea.'

There was the sound of heels click-clacking behind her and Violet turned to see Lorna coming back. 'Silly me. I forgot my phone,' Lorna said and with a sly smile at Cam added, 'Aren't you going to kiss her and let her get back to work?'

Violet sneaked a glance at Cam but instead of looking annoyed at Lorna's comment he smiled an easy smile and reached for Violet's hand and drew her against his side. 'I was just getting to that,' he said.

Violet assumed he would wait till Lorna had gone back into the building before releasing her but Lorna didn't go back into the building. She stood three steps up from them with that annoying smirk on her mouth as if daring Cam to follow through. Cam turned his back to Lorna and slipped a hand under Violet's hair, cupping the nape of her neck, making every nerve beneath her skin pirouette.

'You don't have to do this...' Violet whispered.

Cam brought his mouth down to within a whisker of hers. 'Yes, I do.'

And then he did.

CHAPTER TWO

CAM PRESSED HIS lips to Violet's mouth and a bomb went off in his head, scattering his common sense like flying shrapnel. *What are you doing?* But he didn't want to listen to his conscience. He had wanted to kiss her from the moment he'd walked into that café earlier and now her annoying workmate had given him the perfect excuse to do so. Violet's mouth tasted like a combination of milk and honey, her lips soft and pliable beneath his. He drew her ballerina-like body even closer, his body responding with a fierce rush of blood to his groin. Her small breasts were pressed against his chest, her slim hips against his, her hands gripping the front of his jacket as if she couldn't stand upright without his support. Hell, he was having trouble keeping upright himself, apart from one part of his anatomy.

It's time to stop. You should stop. You need to stop. The chanting of his brain was attempting to drown out the frantic panting of his body. *Yes. Yes. Yes.* Clearly it had been too long between drinks. His self-control was usually spot on. But he didn't want the kiss to end. He felt as though he might *die* if it did. Lust pounded through his body, rampaging, roaring lust that made every cell in his system shudder with need. Intense need. Need that made him think of sweating, straining bodies and tangled sheets and blissful, euphoric release.

She gave a little mewling sound when he shifted position, her mouth flowering open to the hungry glide of his tongue. He explored her sweet interior, his pulse rate going off the scale when her tongue came into play with his. Her tongue was hesitant at first, but then she made another whimpering sound and grew more and more confident, flirting with his tongue, darting away and coming back for the sensual heat of his strokes. He put his hands on her hips, holding her to the throbbing ache of his body.

She felt so damn good, like she was made for his exact proportions. Had he ever felt so aroused so quickly? It was like he was a hormone-driven teenager all over again. He seriously had to get his work/life balance sorted out. How long had it been since he'd slept with a woman? Too long if his trigger was being tripped by just a kiss.

A car tooting on its way past was the only thing

that got through to him. Cam put Violet from him,
holding her by the hands so as to help her keep her
balanced. He did a quick glance over his shoulder
but Violet's workmate had disappeared. Not surprising given he'd lost track of time during that
kiss.

Violet blinked as if trying to reorient herself.
Her small pink tongue did a quick circuit of her
lips and his groin groaned and growled with need.
He could almost imagine how it would feel to
have that shy little tongue move over his body. He
couldn't remember a kiss being so…consuming.
He had forgotten where they were. He had darned
near forgotten who he was. He might be seriously
hot for Violet but he wasn't going to act on it. She
was his best mate's kid sister, the baby of the family he adored.

It was a boundary he was determined not to
cross. Or at least not to cross any further than he
just had.

Cam released her hands and gave a relaxed smile
he hoped disguised the bedlam of base needs in his
body baying for more. 'That was quite a kiss.'

Violet gave him a distracted little smile that
seemed to set off a rippling tide of worry in her
toffee-brown eyes. 'Y-you caught me by surprise…'

Right back at you, sweetheart. 'Yes, well, I figured your workmate wasn't going to go away until we got it over with. Is she usually that persistent?'

'You caught her on a good day.'

Cam wondered how much bullying went on in that office. Violet was a gentle soul who would find it hard to stand up for herself in a dog-eat-dog environment. Even within the loving and loud bosom of her family, she had the tendency to shrink away to a quiet corner rather than engage in the lively banter. Before he could stop himself, he brushed a fingertip down the pinked slope of her cheek. 'You're completely safe with me, Violet. You do know that, don't you? Kissing is all we'll do if the need should arise.' *I hope fate isn't listening, otherwise you are toast.*

Her small white teeth sank into the pillow of her lower lip and she lowered her gaze to a point at the base of his neck. 'Of course.' Her voice was not much more than a scratchy whisper.

He stepped back from her. 'I'd better let you get back to work.'

She turned without another word and climbed the steps, not even glancing back before disappearing into the building when she got to the top.

Cam let out a long breath and walked on. It was all well and good to kiss her but that was as far as it could go. He wasn't what Violet was looking for. He wasn't the settling down type. Maybe one day he would think about setting up a home with someone, but right now he had too much going on in his career. That was his focus, his priority. Not relationships.

Marriage might work for some people, but it didn't work for others—his parents and their collection of exes being a case in point. Too many people got hurt when relationships broke down. It was like a boulder dropped into a pond; the ripples of hurt went on for years. He was still sidestepping the pain his parents' divorce had caused. It wasn't that he'd wanted them to stay together. Far from it. They hadn't been happy from the get-go because his mother had been in love and his father hadn't and then his father had dumped his mother for someone younger and more attractive and had been outrageously difficult about the divorce. His mother had responded by being equally difficult and, inevitably, Cam had got caught up in the middle until eventually he'd been dumped at boarding school and left to fend for himself. In the years since, his parents had changed partners so often Cam had trouble keeping track of names and addresses and birthdays. He'd had to set up a database on his phone to keep on top of them all.

But he needed to get Sophia Nicolaides off his case and taking Violet was the way to do it. Sophia was too crafty to spot a fake. He couldn't bring someone he'd only just met to the dinner. It had to be someone he already felt comfortable with and her with him. Violet was shy around him, but then, she was shy around most people. It was part of her charm, the fact that she didn't flaunt her assets or draw attention to herself. He'd been upfront about the fact it wasn't a date and he was sure she too wouldn't want to compromise the friendship that had built up over the years.

At least they'd got the first kiss out of the way.

And what a kiss. Who knew that sweet little mouth could wreak such havoc on his self-control? He would have to watch himself. Violet wasn't street smart like the women he normally dated. She wasn't the sleep-around type. He wondered if she was still a virgin. Not likely since she was close to thirty, but who knew for sure? It wasn't exactly a question he'd feel comfortable asking her. It was none of his business.

Cam ran his tongue over his lips and tasted her. Even if he never kissed her again, it was going to take a long time to forget that kiss.

If he ever did.

Violet tried on seven different outfits until she finally settled on a navy-blue velvet dress that fell just above the knee. It reminded her of the colour of Cam's unusual eyes. *Maybe that was why you bought it?* No. Of course not. She'd bought it because she liked it. It suited her. She loved the feel of the fabric against her skin. She slipped her feet into heels and turned to view her reflection in the cheval mirror.

Her flatmate, Amy, popped her head around the door. 'Gosh, you look scrumptious. I love that colour on you. Are you going out?'

Violet smoothed the front of her dress over her stomach and thighs, turning this way and that to check if she had visible panty line. No. All good. 'You don't think it's too...plain?'

'It's simple but elegant,' Amy said, perching on the end of Violet's bed. 'So who's the guy? Have I met him? No, of course I haven't because you've never brought anyone here, that I know of.'

Violet slipped on some pearl drop earrings her parents had given her for her twenty-first birthday. 'He's a friend of my brother's. I've known him for ages.' *And he kisses like a sex god and my body is still humming with desire hours later.*

Amy's eyes danced. 'Ooh! A friends-to-lovers thing. How exciting.'

Violet sent her a quelling look. 'Don't get your hopes up. I'm not his type.' Cam couldn't have been more succinct. *'Kissing is all we'll do.'* She hadn't turned him on… Well, she had, but clearly not enough that he wanted to take things further.

The doorbell sounded and Amy jumped off the bed. 'I'll get it. I want to check out your date to see if he passes muster. Flat twenty-three B has certain standards, you know.'

Violet came out a few seconds later to see Amy giving an impression of a star-struck teen in front of a Hollywood idol. Violet had to admit Cam looked heart-stoppingly fabulous in a suit. He wasn't the designer-wear type, but the sharp tailoring of his charcoal-grey suit fitted his tall frame to perfection and the white dress shirt and blue and grey striped tie highlighted the tanned and healthy tone of his skin and the intense blue of his eyes.

Cam's gaze met Violet's and a tiny invisible fist punched her in the stomach.

'You look stunning.' The deep huskiness of his voice was like a caressing stroke down the entire length of her spine. The way his eyes dipped to her lipgloss-coated mouth made her relive every pulse-racing second of that kiss. Was he remembering it too? How it had felt to have their tongues intimately entwined? How it had felt to taste each other, to feel each other's response? How it had felt to end it without the satiation both their bodies craved?

Violet brushed an imaginary strand of hair off her face. 'This is one of my flatmates, Amy Kennedy. Amy, this is Cameron McKinnon, a friend from way back.'

When Cam took Amy's hand, Violet thought her flatmate was going to fall into a swoon. 'Pleased to meet you,' he said.

Amy's cheeks were bright pink and her mouth seemed to be having trouble closing. 'Same.'

Violet picked up her coat and Cam stood behind her and helped her into it. His body was so close she could feel its warmth and smell that intriguing blend of his aftershave. He briefly rested his hands on the tops of her shoulders before stepping away. While he was facing the other way, Amy gave her the thumbs-up sign, eyes bright with excitement. Violet picked up her purse and followed Cam to the door.

'Have a good time!' Amy's voice had a sing-song quality to it that made Violet feel like a teen going out on her first date.

Cam led her to his car, parked a few metres down the rain-slicked street. 'How many flatmates do you have?'

'Two. Amy and Stefanie.'

Violet slipped into the plush leather seat of his showroom-perfect convertible. There was no way she could ever imagine a couple of kids' seats in the back. His car was like his lifestyle—free and fast. Not that he was a hardened playboy or anything. But he was hardly a monk. He was a healthy man of thirty-four, in the prime of his life. Why wouldn't he make the most of his freedom? How many women had experienced that divine mouth? That gorgeous body and all the sensual delights it promised?

Probably more than she wanted to think about.

'I'm sorry about Amy back there,' Violet said after they were on the move. 'She can be a bit over the top.'

Cam glanced her way. 'Did I pass the test?'

Violet could feel an annoying blush creeping over her cheeks. 'The girls have a checklist for potential dates. No smokers, no heavy drinkers, no drugs, no tattoos. Must be gainfully employed, must respect women, must wear a condom... I mean during...you know...not at the time of meeting... That would be ridiculous.'

Cam's deep laugh made the base of her spine quiver. 'Good to know I tick all the boxes.'

Violet swivelled in her seat to look at him. 'So what's on your checklist?'

He appeared to think about it for a moment or maybe it was because he was concentrating on the traffic snarl ahead. 'Nothing specific. Intelligence is always good, a sense of humour.'

'Looks?'

He gave a lip shrug. 'Not as important as other qualities.'

'But you've only ever dated incredibly beautiful women. I've seen photos of them. Fraser showed me.'

'Mere coincidence.'

Violet snorted. 'Well-to-do men are selective when choosing a lover. Women, in general, are much more accepting over looks. It's a well-known fact.'

'What are you looking for in a partner?'

Violet looked at her hands where they were clutching her purse. 'I guess I want what my parents have—a partner who loves me despite my faults and is there for me no matter what.'

'Your parents are a tough act to follow.'

She let out a long sigh. 'Tell me about it.'

The dinner was at a restaurant in Soho. Cam's client had booked a private room and he and his wife were already seated at the table when they arrived. The man rose and greeted Cam warmly. 'So good you could join us. Sophia has been excited about it all day, haven't you, *agapi mou*?'

Sophia was excited all right. Violet could see the sultry gleam in those dark eyes as they roved Cam's body like she was mentally undressing him.

Cam's arm was around Violet's waist. 'Nick and Sophia Nicolaides, this is my partner Violet. Darling, this is Nick and Sophia.'

Partner? What was wrong with girlfriend? Partner sounded a little more…permanent. But then he wanted to make sure Sophia got the message loud and clear. 'Darling' was a nice touch, however. Violet quite liked that. No one had ever called her that before. She got 'poppet' and 'wee one' from her parents and her grandad called her Vivi like her siblings did. 'I'm very pleased to meet you both,' she said. 'Cam's told me all about you. Are you in London long?'

'Until New Year,' Nick said. 'Sophia's never had an English Christmas before.'

Sophia looked like all her Christmases and New Year's Eves had come at once when she slid her hand through Cam's arm. 'You're a dark horse, aren't you?' she said. 'You never told us you had a partner. Are you engaged?'

Cam's smile looked a little tight around the edges as he disentangled himself from Sophia's tentacle-like arm. 'Not yet.'

Not yet? Didn't that imply he was actually considering it? Violet had trouble keeping her expression composed. Even though she knew he was only saying it for the sake of appearances, her heart still gave an excited little leap. Not that she was in love with him or anything. She was just imagining what it would be like if she was. How it would feel to have him look at her with that tender look he was sending her way and actually mean it. For real.

Sophia smiled but it didn't crease her eyes at the corners, although that could have been because of Botox. *Meow.* Violet wasn't normally the critical type but something about the predatory nature of Nick Nicolaides' wife irritated her beyond measure. Sophia looked like the type of woman for whom the word 'no' was a challenge rather than an obstacle. What Sophia wanted, Sophia got. No matter what. And Sophia wanted Cam. It was a wonder Nick couldn't see it. Or was Nick so enamoured with his young, stunningly beautiful wife he couldn't see what was right before his eyes?

Violet decided it was time to draw the line, not in sand but in concrete. She gazed up at Cam with what she hoped passed for besotted devotion. 'I didn't know you were thinking along those lines this early in our relationship.'

He leaned down and dropped a kiss to her upturned mouth. 'It's never too early to say I love you.'

Violet smiled a blissfully happy smile. Who said she couldn't act? Or maybe she wasn't acting. Hearing him say those words, even though deep down she knew he didn't mean them, had a potent effect on her. No one, apart from her family, had told her they loved her. 'I love you, too, baby.' She turned her smile up a notch.

Nick slapped Cam on the shoulder. 'Let's have a drink to celebrate in advance of the announcement.'

Champagne was ordered and served and the glasses held up in a toast to an engagement that wasn't going to happen. It felt weird to be part of such a deception but Violet had no choice but to run with it. Sophia kept looking at her, sizing her up as if wondering what on earth Cam saw in her. Violet didn't let it intimidate her, which was surprising as, under normal circumstances, she would have retreated to the trenches by now.

Dinner was a long, drawn-out affair because Nick wanted to discuss business with Cam, which left Violet to make conversation with Sophia. Never good at small talk, Violet had exhausted her twenty question checklist before the entrées were cleared away.

Cam came to her rescue after what was left of their mains was removed. He excused them both from the table and escorted her out to the restroom. 'You're doing great, Violet. Hang in there.'

'If looks could kill, I'd be lying in a morgue with a tag on my big toe right about now,' Violet said through clenched teeth. 'She is *such* a cow. She's not even trying to hide how she's lusting after you. Why can't Nick see it? She's so brazen it's nauseating.'

Cam's mouth was set in a grim line. 'I think he does see it but he's in denial. I don't want to be the one to take the bullet for pointing it out to him. This project is too important to me. It's the biggest contract I've done and more could follow. Nick has a lot of contacts. Word of mouth is everything in my business.'

Violet studied his tense features for a moment. 'If she weren't married would she be the type of woman you'd be involved with?'

'God, no.' His tone was adamant. 'What sort of man do you think I am?'

'She's incredibly beautiful.'

'So are you.'

Violet moistened her lips. 'You're terrifyingly good at lying.'

His brows came together. 'You think I'm lying? Don't you have mirrors at your flat? You turned every head when you walked through the main restaurant just now.'

Keep it light. Violet smiled a teasing smile to cover her self-consciousness. Compliments had never been her strong point. She knew it was polite to accept them with thanks but she could never quite pull it off with sophisticated aplomb. And if people noticed her when she came into a room, she never saw it. She was always too busy keeping her head down trying *not* to be noticed. 'You *were* lying about the intended proposal.'

His dark blue eyes held hers in a lock that made the base of her spine tingle like sherbet. 'I can be ruthless when it comes to nailing a business deal, but not that ruthless.'

'Good to know.'

His phone pinged with an incoming message. His expression turned sour when he checked the screen.

'Sophia?' Violet's tone was incredulous. 'She texted you while her husband is sitting right next to her?'

Cam expelled a breath and pocketed his phone. 'Go and powder your nose, I'll wait for you here.'

Cam led Violet back to the private dining room. She had reapplied her lipgloss and it made her lips all the more tempting to kiss. *Get a grip.* This was an act, not the real deal. He wasn't interested in the real deal. Not with anyone just now and particularly not with a girl he had viewed as a surrogate sister for the last twelve years.

But then last Easter something had changed.

He had changed.

He had suddenly noticed her. As in *noticed* her. The way she smiled that shy smile that made the corners of her mouth tilt upwards and then quiver, as if uncertain whether to stay there or not. The way she bit her lower lip when she was nervous. The way she moved her body like a graceful dancer. Her beautiful brown eyes that reminded him of caramel. Her creamy skin with that tiny dusting of freckles over the bridge of her nose that he found adorable.

Adorable?

Okay, time to rein it in. He had no right to be thinking about her that way. If he crossed the boundary any further it had the potential to ruin his relationship with her whole family. Three generations of it. He had so many wonderful memories of spending time at Drummond Brae, the big old house set on a Highland estate just out of Inverness. He had met Fraser Drummond in his fourth year at university in London when they were both twenty-two. It felt like a lifetime ago now.

But he still remembered the first time he had visited the Drummond family. It was nothing like any of the families he had been a part of, his nuclear family in particular. He had been struck by their warmth, the way they loved and accepted each other; the easygoing bonhomie between them was something he had never witnessed outside of a television show. Sure, they argued, but no one shouted or swore obscenities or threw things or stormed out in a huff. No one went through an insanely bitter divorce and then refused to have the other person's name mentioned in their presence ever again. Violet's parents were as in love with each other as the first day they'd met. Their solid relationship was the backbone of the family, the scaffolding providing the safety net of stability that allowed each sibling to grow to their full potential. Even the way Margie Drummond was taking care of her ill ninety-year-old father-in-law Archie was indicative of the unconditional love that flowed in the family.

Cam had become an ancillary part of that family in a way he wouldn't dream of compromising, even if it meant ignoring the persistent drumbeat of lust he had going on for Violet—the baby of the clan. Who was doing an excellent job of pretending to be in love with him at the moment.

But it was far more than the fear of compromising his relationship with her family that held him back. How could he even think about settling down when he was all over the place with work commitments? He was driven to succeed and the only way to succeed was to put everything else on hold. Work was his focus. His first priority. His only priority. If he got distracted now, he could jeopardise everything he'd worked so hard for since the day he'd been left at boarding school. He was used to being an island. Self-sufficient.

Violet resumed her seat next to Cam at the table and looped her slim arm through his, gazing up at him with those big brown eyes as if she thought the world began and ended and only made sense with him. This close he could smell her perfume, a bewitching combination of spring flowers that tantalised his senses until he felt slightly drunk. Or mad. Definitely mad. Mad with lust. He could feel it pounding in his pelvis when she leaned closer, her slim pale hand sliding down to his.

Her touch should not be having this effect on him. He was not a lust-crazed teenager. Normally he could control himself. But if she looked at his lap right now, he'd have some explaining to do. He still had some explaining to do after that kiss. He had been hard for her with one kiss. One kiss, for God's sake! What sort of tragic did that make him? Yes, he hadn't had sex in a while but he'd been busy since Easter... And no, it had nothing to do with seeing

Violet that weekend. Nothing to do with noticing her in a way he had never done before.

Or had it?

Had he not pursued the many opportunities he'd had for a casual fling because something had gnawed at him since Easter? The sense that there had to be something more…something more than a few drinks or dinners, a few mostly satisfactory tumbles and a 'goodbye, thanks for the memories'?

For years he had been perfectly content with his lifestyle. He enjoyed the freedom to take on extra work without the pressure of being responsible for someone's emotional upkeep. He had seen both of his parents struggle and fail to meet the needs of each other and their subsequent partners whilst juggling the demands of a career and family. It had always looked like too much hard work.

But there was something to be said for feeling something more than basic lust for a sexual partner. Kissing Violet had felt…different somehow. The connection they had as long-term friends had brought a completely different dynamic to the kiss. He couldn't quite explain it. Maybe he would have to kiss her again… *There's a thought.*

'Smile for the camera,' Sophia said from the other side of the table, holding up her phone.

Cam smiled and leaned his head against Violet's

fragrant one, her hair tickling his cheek, her closeness doing something dangerous to his hormones. The photo was taken and Sophia sat back with a Cheshire cat smile. He didn't trust that smile. He didn't trust that woman. He didn't trust his deal with Nick would be secure until the contract was signed, sealed and delivered. But Nick was dragging things out a bit. This trip to London was obviously part of the stalling campaign. Cam couldn't help feeling he was being subjected to some sort of test. Maybe Nick knew exactly what his flirty young wife was up to but wanted to see how Cam would deal with it.

He was dealing with it just fine. With Violet's help. But how long would he have to play pretend? This weekend was fine. But after that? There was only one more week before Christmas. If word got out… His gut seized at the thought. Why had he got himself into this? Seeing Violet in that café earlier had been purely coincidence.

Or had it?

He had felt drawn to that café as if a navigational device inside his body had taken him there. When he'd seen her sitting there all alone something had shifted inside him. Like a gear going up a notch. He had gone from *noticing her* to wanting her…as in *wanting* her. He had offered to take her to the party not because he felt sorry for her but because he couldn't bear the thought of some sleazy colleague trying it on with her.

Green-eyed monster?

You bet.

CHAPTER THREE

VIOLET WASN'T SURE she liked the idea of Sophia having photos of her and Cam but what could she do? She had to play along and pretend everything was fine. Thing was, it *felt* fine. Leaning against him, smiling up at him, looking into those amazingly blue eyes of his that crinkled up at the corners when he smiled—all of it felt so fine she had trouble remembering this was all an act. That it wasn't going to last beyond the weekend.

'Nick and I are going to dance at the nightclub down the road,' Sophia said. 'Come and join us.'

It wasn't an invitation—it was a command. One Violet would have ignored but for the forty million pounds that were hanging in the balance.

And because she didn't want Sophia to think she was one bit intimidated by her. It was how mean girls worked. They manipulated and caused trouble, striking mischief-making matches and standing back to watch the explosion like Lorna had done outside the office.

But there was another reason Violet walked into that nightclub on Cam's arm. She had never danced with anyone. Not since that party. She hated the crush of bodies. The threat of strangers touching her, even by accident as they jostled on the dance floor, had always been too threatening.

But if she danced with Cam it would prove she was moving on. Taking back the control she had lost. She had never danced with him, not even at one of her family's famous *ceilidhs*. He had always refrained from joining into the fun, citing the fact that he had no coordination or wasn't a true Scot and there was no way he was ever wearing a skirt. But this would be the perfect opportunity to get him on the dance floor. A legitimate excuse to be in his arms. Where she felt safe.

But Violet hadn't factored in the music. It wasn't the swaying-in-your-partner's-arms sort. It was loud, an auditory assault that made conversation other than sign language virtually impossible. The nightclub dance floor was cramped with sweaty, gyrating bodies. It was exactly the sort of place she normally avoided. There wasn't room to swing a cat, let alone a dance partner.

But Sophia and Nick seemed to be enjoying every eardrum-splitting moment. They were jigging about, weaving their way through the knot of dancers as if they did it every day of the week. They waved to Cam and Violet on their way past, shouting over the music, 'Come and join us!'

Violet looked up at Cam, who looked like he was suffering from indigestion. She stepped up on tiptoe and cupped her hand around his ear. 'Are you going to ask me to dance? Because, if so, let me spare you the embarrassment of being rejected.'

'You call that dancing?'

A smile tugged at her mouth and she stepped up to his ear again. 'You ever get the feeling you were born into the wrong century? Give me a traditional Gay Gordon dance any day.'

He drew her closer in a quick squeeze hug that made her breath hitch. 'I feel about a hundred and fifty in here.'

'Age or temperature?'

He gave a crooked smile and took out his handkerchief—*why did classy men always have one?*—and gently blotted the beads of perspiration that had gathered on her forehead. Violet couldn't tear her eyes away from the deep steady focus of his. What was he thinking behind the screen of his gaze? His eyes dipped to her mouth, his lashes going to half-mast, giving him a sexily hooded look that made her belly quiver like someone bumping into an unset bowl of jelly. She moistened her mouth...not because it was dry but because she liked seeing him watch her do so. He moved closer, his thighs strong and muscular, so very male against her trembling legs. She felt the ridge of his arousal. It should have shocked her, would've shocked her, if it had been anyone else.

But it was Cam.

Who desired her even though he didn't want to. It was a force they were both fighting...for different reasons. Violet didn't want to waste time in a relationship going nowhere even if it was with the most desirable man she had ever met. Cam wasn't interested in finding a life partner. He didn't want to be tied down to family life. Understandable, given the atrocious example his parents had set. But Violet couldn't help wondering if deep down he was less concerned about his loss of freedom and more concerned about not being the sort of husband and father he most aspired to be. He was a perfectionist. Doing a good job wasn't enough for someone like Cam. If he put his mind and energy to something he did it brilliantly. That was why he was one of the most celebrated naval architects in the world.

'Let's go someplace else,' Cam said against her ear.

Had he suggested leaving because he knew she was uncomfortable in that environment? Violet couldn't help but be touched by his concern. 'But what about Nick and—?'

'They'll survive without us.' He took her hand and led her out of the nightclub. 'I'll send Nick a text to say we had to leave. He'll think I want to whip you away somewhere private.'

Please do! Violet followed him out of the nightclub to the wet and cold street outside. Within a few minutes they were in the warm cocoon of his car. But instead of driving her back to her flat he turned in the direction of his house in Belgravia. She hadn't been there before…although she'd walked past. Purely to satisfy her feminine interest, of course. During the drive he'd suggested a nightcap, which could have been code for something else but she took it at face value. Besides, going back to her flat, which would be empty now because both Amy and Stef had steady boyfriends and spent most weekends at their homes, was not the most exciting prospect.

Violet had to pretend to be surprised by the outside of the house when he pulled up in front of it. 'Is this your place? Wow! It's gorgeous. How long have you had it? It looks massive.'

'I bought it a year or so ago.' He led her up the black and white tiled pathway to the front door. 'I've done most of the renovations myself.'

Violet knew he was good with his hands; she had the humming body to prove it. But she hadn't realised he was a handyman of this sort of standard. The house was amazing. A showcase similar to those you would see in a home and lifestyle magazine. It was a three storey high Georgian mansion with beautiful features throughout. Crystal chandeliers tinkled above when Cam closed the door against the wintry breeze. The plush Persian carpet runner that led the way down the wide hallway threatened to swallow Violet's feet whole. The antique furniture made her mouth water. Some girls loved fashion and jewellery but anything old and precious did it for her. There were priceless works of art on the walls in gilt-edged frames. Sculptures on marble stands, a white orchid in full bloom on another softening the overall effect.

Cam led her through to a sitting room with a fireplace with a stunning black marble surround with brass trim. Twin cream sofas, deep as a cloud, sat opposite each other with a mahogany coffee table in between. A Louis XV chair was featured in one corner next to a small cedar writing desk next to a full bookcase. It looked like the perfect room for curling up with a book…or cuddling up with the one you loved.

Stop it. You're letting it go to your head.

Violet realised then with a little jolt that this was the first time they had been completely alone. At Drummond Brae there had always been members of her family about the place, if not in the same room. She had never truly been alone with Cam without the threat of interruption.

Violet turned from taking in all of the room to find him looking at her with an unreadable expression. The air seemed to tighten and then to crackle as if an invisible current was being transmitted through their gazes. She could feel her body responding to the magnetic presence of his. She was half a room away but it felt like a force was drawing her to him, a force she could not control even if she wanted to. 'Why are you looking at me like that?' she asked, barely recognising the breathy voice as coming from her.

'How am I looking at you?'

'As if you don't want me to know what you're thinking.'

His mouth lifted in a wry smile that tugged on

something deep inside her. 'Believe me, you don't want to know what I'm thinking.'

'Try me.' *Did you just say that? Isn't that flirting? That thing you never do?*

He closed the distance in a couple of strides, standing close enough for her to feel the potent energy of his body calling out to hers. 'This is all sorts of crazy.' He didn't touch her. He just stood there looking down at her with that inscrutable expression on his face.

Violet disguised a tiny swallow. 'What is?'

She heard him draw in a breath, it sounded as if it caught on something on the way through. He lifted his hand, brushing the backs of his bent fingers down the slope of her cheek. 'Being alone with you. It's...ill-advised.'

Ill-advised? Violet wondered what other word he'd considered using. Dangerous? Tempting? Inevitable? All three seemed to apply. She looked at his mouth, knowing it was a signal for him to kiss her. Knowing it and doing it anyway. It was what she wanted. It was what he wanted. She might not be very experienced but she could tell when a man wanted to kiss a woman.

She lowered her lashes over her eyes, swaying towards him. *Kiss me. Kiss me. Kiss me.* She placed her hands on the wall of his chest. The feel of his firm male form beneath her palms sent a thrill through her body. It was like being plugged into a power source. She felt the sensual voltage from her palms to the balls of her feet…and other places. Places she mostly ignored, but not now. Her feminine core responded to his closeness with a tight, clenching ache. His head came down, his mouth hovering within a breath of hers as if some fraying thread of self-control was only just keeping him in check.

Violet took matters into her own hands…or mouth, so to speak. She closed the minuscule distance by placing her lips to his, her heart kicking in excitement when he made a low, deep groaning sound before he took charge of the kiss. His lips were firmer than the last time, not rough but with an undercurrent of desperation as if the self-control he had always relied on had finally let him down. She felt it in the way his tongue came in ruthless search of hers, tangling with it in an erotic dance that made her skin pop all over with goose bumps. The spread of his fingers through her hair made every nerve on her scalp tingle at the roots, his mouth continuing its sensual teasing until she was mindless with longing. His stubble grazed her cheek and then her chin but she didn't care. This was what she'd been hungering for all evening…or maybe for most of her adult life.

* * *

The insistent sound of her phone vibrating and chir-ruping from within her evening bag would have been easy to ignore under normal circumstances, but it was late at night. Late night phone calls usu-ally meant something was wrong. And with her frail grandfather it was hard not to worry something ter-rible had happened. Violet eased back from Cam's embrace and gave him a wincing look. 'Sorry, bet-ter answer that. It might be urgent.'

'Sure.' He rubbed a hand over the back of his neck and stood back while she fished her phone out of her purse.

By the time Violet got her phone out it had stopped, but she frowned when she saw she'd missed six calls from her mother. There were three each from all of her siblings. Her stomach dropped like an elevator with sabotaged cables. She pressed speed dial and looked at Cam with a grimace as she braced herself for bad news.

'Mum? What's wrong? You called me—'

'Poppet, why didn't you tell me?' Her mother's clear voice carried as if Violet had put her on speaker. 'It's all over social media. I've had everyone calling to confirm it. We're so delighted for you and Cam. When did he ask you? Tell me everything. It's just so exciting! Grandad's taken on a new lease of life.

He got out of bed and had a wee dram to celebrate. He says he's going to make it to your wedding and no one's going to stop him. Your father's beside himself with joy. Here, speak to him.'

Violet looked wide-eyed at Cam for help, mouthing, *What will I say?*

Cam gestured for her to hand him the phone. He took it and held it to his ear, his eyes on Violet's, his expression was calm on the surface, but she could see a tiny muscle in his jaw going on and off like a miniature hammer. 'Gavin? Yes, well, we were hoping to keep it quiet a little longer but—'

'Congratulations,' her father said. 'Couldn't have asked for a better son-in-law. You have my every blessing, Cam. You're already a big part of the family—this has just made it formal. You and our little Vivi. I'm so thrilled I can barely tell you. I know you'll look after our baby girl.'

After a few more effusive congratulations from both her parents, Cam handed back the phone to Violet and she was subjected to the same. This was the trouble with having parents who were enthusiastic and encouraging in anything and everything their children did. There was barely a space for her to put a word in. Finally her parents ended the call and Violet switched her phone off. Her siblings would be next. There would be another barrage of verbiage she wouldn't be able to contradict for fear of disappointing everyone.

But her brother and sisters would have to wait until she figured out what Cam was up to. Why hadn't he denied it? Why let it continue when so many people would be hurt when the truth came out?

'Okay, so apparently we're now engaged,' she said, shooting him a *please explain* look. 'Any idea how that happened?'

His mouth was set in a rigid line. 'Sophia Nicolaides must have made an announcement on social media with that photo she took of us at dinner. Do you know how many followers she has?' He turned away and let out a stiff curse. 'I should've known something like this would happen.'

'But we could've just denied it.'

He swung his gaze back to hers. 'You heard what your mother said. Your grandfather practically came out of a coma at the news. No, we'll have to run with it—at least until after Christmas.'

Violet's heart was doing a rather good impression of having some sort of medical event. 'Why till after Christmas?'

'Because I don't want your family's Christmas to be spoilt,' he said. 'It's the time when everyone comes together. Your mother puts such a lot of effort into making it special for everyone. Can you imagine how awkward it would be if we were to tell them it's all a lie?'

Violet chewed her lip. He was right. Of course he was. Christmas was a big thing in her family and it would be ruined if she and Cam put them straight about the charade they were playing. And surely poor old Grandad deserved to have his last Christmas as happy as they could make it? It wasn't like Cam was going to keep this going for ever. He didn't want to settle down. The last thing he would want to do was tie himself down with a woman he wasn't in love with. He liked her, loved her even in a platonic sort of way, but he wasn't in love with her. She wasn't his type. She wasn't anyone's type.

'But we're going to have to tell them some time...'

Cam dragged a hand down his face, momentarily distorting his handsome features. 'I know, but there's too much at stake. And no, I'm not just referring to this deal with Nicolaides.'

'Apart from my family, what else is at stake?'

He let out a ragged-sounding breath. 'There's my family for one thing. I'm not sure I want to show up to my father's fifth wedding on Christmas Eve with a broken engagement under my belt. He'll never let me hear the end of it. I can hear everyone saying it now. *Like father, like son.*'

Violet could understand his point of view. From what she knew of his father, Ross McKinnon would make the most of any opportunity to rub in Cam's mistakes as a way to take the focus off his own behaviour. His mother, Candice, would also not let a chance like that go by, given Cam had been so critical of how both his parents had behaved over the years.

'Right, well, it looks like we run with it then.'

At least her office Christmas party would be less of an ordeal with him there as her fiancé. For once she would be spared the sleazy flirting from male colleagues, and at least there would be no more pitying looks from some of the women who thought it fine sport to make a mockery out of her being single. It was a win-win…she hoped.

Cam picked up his keys from the writing desk where he'd left them earlier. 'I'd better take you home. It's late.'

Violet's spirits slumped in disappointment. Didn't he want to finish the kiss they'd started? 'I don't have to be back by any set time,' she said. 'The girls are sleeping over at their boyfriends' so…'

His sober expression halted her speech. 'Violet.' The way he said her name with that deep note of gravity was a little disquieting to say the least. 'We're not going there, okay?'

There? Where was 'there'? All she wanted was a little more kissing and…a little fooling around. Okay, *lots* of fooling around. Violet forced a smile.

He looked at her for a long moment, his eyes moving back and forth between each of hers in a searching manner that made her feel like someone was trickling sand down the column of her spine. 'I said we'd kiss and that's all.'

'Fine. No problem. Best to be sensible about this.' The words kept tumbling out. 'Way, way too awkward if we go there. I'm not your type in any case. Not enough experience for one thing.'

His brows formed a bridge over his dark-as-midnight blue eyes. 'How much experience have you had?'

Violet gave a self-deprecating grimace. 'Well… let's put it this way. I haven't been around the block, I got to the corner and then got kind of lost.'

His frown deepened. 'What do you mean?'

What are you doing? You haven't ever told anyone about…that.

Violet pressed her lips together, wondering if she should go any further. Would it make him see her differently? Make him judge her for being a naïve little fool to get into such a situation? But something about his concerned expression made her realise he would be the last person to pass judgement on her. 'I'd rather not talk about it…'

'You can tell me, Violet.' Cam's voice was so steady, so strong, so calm. But then he had always been a good listener. Violet remembered an occasion during her teens when she'd found herself telling him about the mean girls at school who had taunted her for not wearing the right label of clothes to a party. *What was it with her and parties?* Cam had listened to her frustrated rant and then assured her the girls were probably jealous because she didn't need designer wear to look gorgeous. Violet remembered blushing to the roots of her hair but feeling a strange sense of warmth every time she recalled that conversation since.

Telling him about what happened at that university party was not on the same level of having a moan about a bunch of vacuous schoolgirls at a teenage birthday bash. Telling him about the trauma of her first sexual experience would be laying herself bare. Opening old wounds that had never properly healed. But there was something about Cam that gave her new strength. Maybe it was time to get it off her chest so she could breathe without that lingering pinching feeling of shame.

'During my first year at university, I went to a party…' She took a short breath before continuing.

'I was trying to fit in instead of being on the outer all the time. I had a couple of drinks—too many drinks, really...'

Violet glanced up to see him frowning so intensely his eyebrows met over his eyes. But it wasn't a frown of disapproval or judgement, it was one of raw concern. It gave her the courage to continue. 'Things got a little hazy and I...well, I woke up and there were three...' She took a painful swallow. 'At first I wasn't sure if it was a dream—a nightmare or something. I was on a bed and there was a man, not someone I knew...'

'Did he...rape you?' Cam's voice came out sounding rusty as if he had trouble getting the words through his throat.

This time Violet couldn't quite meet his gaze but aimed it at a point just below his chin. 'I'm not sure... I don't remember that part. Can you call it rape if you don't remember anything? There wasn't just one man... I'm not sure if they were just... watching or...'

He took her by the hands and drew her close but not quite touching his body as if he was worried about making her feel uncomfortable after her confession. 'Did you report it?'

Violet shook her head. 'I couldn't bear anyone knowing about it. I didn't tell anyone, not even

Mum or Rose or Lily. I felt so ashamed I'd got myself into that situation. I just locked it away and… and, well, I quit my studies. I couldn't help feeling people were looking at me differently around the campus…you know? I just thought it best to move on and pretend it never happened.'

He drew her against him in a gentle hug, resting his head on top of hers. 'I wish I'd been at that party because there's no way those lowlife creeps would have got away with that.' The deep resonance of his voice from his chest where it was pressed against hers was a strange sort of comfort. She felt safe in a way she hadn't felt in years. If only he had been there. If only she had been able to run to him and have him hold her, protect her. He was that type of man. Honourable. Chivalrous. There was no way he would spike anyone's drink and take advantage of a woman when she was too out of it to give proper consent. The world needed more men like Cam. Men who weren't afraid to stand up to bullies. Men who were brave and steadfast in their values. Men who treated women as equals and not as objects to service their needs.

Violet looked up at him. 'Thank you.'

He gently stroked her hair back from her face. 'It wasn't your fault, Violet. What those men did was wrong. You're not the one who should be feeling

ashamed. They committed a crime and so did anyone else at that party who witnessed it and didn't
report it.'

'I was so worried there might be…photos…'

He winced as if someone had stabbed him in the
gut. 'Do you remember anyone taking any?'

Violet shook her head. 'No, but there was so
much I didn't remember so I could never be sure
one way or the other. It's made the humiliation of
that night go on and on. For ten years I've worried
someone out there has photos of me…like that, and
I can't do anything about it.'

Cam's expression was tight with rage on her behalf. There were white tips around his mouth and
his jaw was locked. 'Think of it this way. If photos
were to surface they could be used as evidence in
court. You could identify the perpetrators and lay
charges.'

Violet hadn't thought of it that way and it was
like a weight coming off her, like taking off a heavy
backpack after a long, exhausting walk. She leaned
her head against his chest, breathing in the clean
male scent of him. He continued to stroke her head,
gentle soothing strokes that made her feel as if she
was the most precious person in the world instead
of someone dirty, tainted, someone to be used for
sport and cast aside.

Violet didn't know how long they stood there like that. It could have been seconds, minutes or even half an hour. All she knew was it felt as if she had come to a safe anchorage after years of tossing about in an unpredictable sea.

But finally he eased back from her, still holding her, his thumbs rhythmically stroking the backs of her hands. 'I want you to know something, Violet. You will always be safe with me. Always.'

Violet wasn't sure she wanted to be safe. The feelings she had for him were dangerous. Dangerous and exciting. 'Thanks...' *I think*. 'But please, I'd rather you didn't mention this to my family. I want to put it behind me. For good.'

'Am I the only person you've told?'

Violet nodded. 'Weird, huh? You of all people.'

His frown was still pleating his forehead. 'Why me of all people?'

She shifted her gaze. 'I don't know... I never thought I'd tell you. I guess I didn't want you to think of me...like that.'

He brought her chin up so her gaze came back to his. 'Hey.' His eyes were as dark as sapphires, his voice low and deep as a bass chord. 'I could never think of you like that and nor should you think of yourself that way. You're a beautiful person who had an ugly thing happen to her. Don't keep punishing yourself.'

Violet had spent years berating herself for being in the wrong place at the wrong time with the wrong personality. If she'd been less reserved, less trusting, more able to stand up for herself, then maybe it wouldn't have happened. For so long she had blamed herself for allowing herself to get into such a situation. But now that she had opened up to Cam, she could see how futile that blame game was. It was time to let it go and accept that it could have happened to anyone. She had been that *anyone* that fateful day.

Violet looked into his dark, caring eyes. Did this mean it was still hands-off? She still wanted him to kiss her. She wanted to be free from her past and experience being in a relationship with a man who respected her and treated her as an equal. Why couldn't Cam be that man? Cam who listened to her as if she were the only person in the world he wanted to hear talk. Cam, whom she'd trusted enough to tell her most shameful secret to, which, strangely enough, didn't feel so shameful now that she had shared it with him.

Cam's phone started ringing and he took it out of his pocket and grimaced when he saw the caller

ID. 'Fraser.' He pressed the mute button. 'I'll call him later.'

Violet bit down on her lip. Fraser wouldn't give up in a hurry. She had yet to talk to him and her sisters. How soon before one of her family began to suspect things weren't quite as they seemed? What if it jeopardised Cam's contract? She didn't want to be responsible for ruining that for him, but nor did she want to be responsible for wrecking everyone's Christmas. 'This situation between us is getting awfully complicated… I'm not a very good liar. What if someone guesses this isn't for real?'

His hand cupped one side of her face, his touch gentle fire licking at her flesh. 'No one will guess. You're doing a great job so far.'

That's because I'm not sure I'm still pretending.

CHAPTER FOUR

CAM DROVE VIOLET back to her flat half an hour later. He was still getting his head around what she'd told him earlier. He'd had trouble containing his rage at what had happened to her. The frustrated anger at the way she had been treated gnawed at him. He had the deepest respect for women and felt sickened to his gut that there were men out there who would act so unconscionably. For all these years since, Violet had lived with the shame of being in the wrong place at the wrong time with the wrong people. It saddened him to think she blamed herself. *Still* blamed herself. No wonder she had no dating life to speak of. Why would she want to fraternise with men if she didn't know if she could trust them?

He didn't trust himself around her. Not that he would ever do anything she didn't want, but still. The attraction that had flared up between them was something he was doing his best to ignore. It was all very well pretending to be engaged for a couple of weeks. Kissing and holding hands and stuff was fine to add a little authenticity. More than fine. But taking it any further?

Not a good idea.

A dumb idea.

An idea that had unfortunately taken root in his brain and was winding its tentacles throughout his body like a rampant vine. He had only to look at Violet and those tentacles of lust coiled and tightened in his groin.

But how could he act on it? Even if it was what she wanted? It wouldn't be fair to her to get her hopes up that he could offer her anything more than a casual relationship. He hated hurting people. If he broke Violet's heart he would never forgive himself. Her family would never forgive him either.

Engaged via social media.

What a nightmare. How had he got himself into such a complicated mess?

Cam walked Violet to the door of her flat but when they got there it was slightly ajar. She stopped dead, cannoning back against his body standing just behind her. 'Oh, no…' Her voice came out as a shocked gasp.

Cam put his hands on her shoulders. 'What's

wrong?' And then he saw what she had seen. The lock had been jemmied open, the woodwork around it splintered. 'Don't touch anything,' he said, moving her out of the way. 'I'll call the police.'

Within a few minutes the police arrived and investigated the scene. The police told Cam and Violet that several flats in the area had been targeted that night in the hunt for drugs and cash. Once they were allowed inside, Cam held Violet's hand as she inspected the mess. And it was a mess. Clothes, shoes, books, kitchen items and even food thrown around and ground into the carpet as if the intruders were intent on causing as much mayhem as possible.

Cam could sense Violet's distress even though she was putting on a brave face. Her bottom lip was quivering and her brown eyes were moving from one scattered item to the next as if wondering how on earth she would ever restore order to the place. He was wondering that himself. 'I... I've got to call Amy and Stef,' she said in a distracted tone, fumbling for her phone in her purse and almost dropping it when she found it.

Cam would have led her to the sofa to sit down but it had been slashed with a sharp object, presumably one of the kitchen knives the police had since bagged and taken away for fingerprinting. He shuddered at the thought of what might have happened if Violet had been alone inside the flat when the intruders broke in. Who knew what this new class of criminals were capable of these days? It didn't bear thinking about. He picked up an overturned chair instead and set it down, making sure it was clean first. 'Here, sweetie. Come and sit down and I'll call the girls for you.'

Violet's expression was a mixture of residual fear and gratitude. 'Would you? I'm not sure I can think straight, let alone talk to anyone just now.'

Cam spoke to both of Violet's flatmates, telling them what had happened and that everything was under control now as he was organising an emergency locksmith to repair the lock. 'And don't worry about Violet,' he added. 'I'm taking her back to my place.'

Of course he would have to take her home with him. There was no question about it. He couldn't leave her in the trashed flat to lie awake all night in terror of being invaded again. Or worse. It was the right thing to do to take her home with him. What friend wouldn't offer a bed for a night or two? He wasn't one for sleepovers. He liked his space too much. But this was Violet. A friend from way back.

It was a pity his body wasn't so clear on the

friend factor, but still. His hormones would have to get control of themselves.

While the locksmith was working on the lock, one of Violet's elderly neighbours shuffled along the corridor to speak to her. 'Are you all right, Violet?' the wizened old man said. 'I didn't hear a thing. The sleeping pills the doctor gave me knock me out for most of the night.'

Violet gave the old man a reassuring smile. 'I'm fine, Mr Yates. I'm glad you weren't disturbed. How's your chest feeling? Is your bronchitis better?'

Cam thought it typical of Violet to be more concerned about her elderly neighbour than herself. The old man gave her a sheepish look. 'The doc reckons I should give up smoking but at my age what other pleasures are there?' He turned his rheumy gaze to Cam. 'And who might you be, young man?'

'I'm Violet's—'

'Friend,' Violet said before Cam could finish his sentence.

Mr Yates's bushy brows waggled. 'Boyfriend?'

'Fiancé, actually,' Cam said with a ridiculous sense of pride he couldn't account for or explain. He knew it was beneath him to be beating his chest in front of an elderly man like some sort of Tarzan figure but he couldn't help it. *Boyfriend* sounded so…juvenile, and *lover*, well, that was even worse. Violet wasn't the sort of girl to take a lover.

Mr Yates smiled a nicotine-stained smile. 'Congratulations. You've got a keeper there in Violet. She's the nicest of the girls who live here. Never could understand why she hasn't been snapped up well before now. You're a lucky man.'

'I know.'

Once the locksmith had finished and Mr Yates had shuffled back to his flat, Cam led Violet back out to his car with a small collection of her belongings to see her through for a few days. Not that she could bring much as most of it had been thrown about the flat. The thought of putting on clothes that some stranger had touched would be horrifying for her. It was horrifying to him.

He glanced at her once they were on their way. She was sitting with a hunched posture, her fingers plucking at her evening bag, her face white and pinched. 'How are you doing?'

'I don't know how to thank you…' She gave a little hiccupping sound as if she was fighting back a sob. 'You've been so amazing tonight. I really don't know what I would've done without you.'

Cam reached for her hand and placed it on top of his thigh. 'That's what friends—or rather, fake fiancés—are for.' His attempt at humour didn't quite hit the mark. Her teeth sank into her lower lip so hard he was worried she would puncture the skin. She looked so tiny and vulnerable it made his chest sting. It made him think of how she must have been after that wretched party—alone, terrified, shocked, with no one she felt she could turn to. If only he had known. If only he had been there that night, he could have done something to protect her. Violet was the sort of girl who made him want to rush off for a white horse and a suit of armour. Her trust in him made him feel…conflicted, truth be told.

He wanted to protect her, sure, but he wanted her, period. Which was a whole lot of capital *T* trouble he could do without right now. Bringing her home with him was the right thing to do. Of course it was. Sure, he could have set her up in a hotel but he sensed she needed company. Her parents were too far away in Scotland to get to her in a hurry, so too were her brother and sisters, who lived in various parts of the country.

Cam was on knight duty so it was up to him to hold her hand.

As long as that's all you hold.

Violet had held off tears only because Cam had done everything that needed to be done. He'd taken charge in a way that made her feel supported and safe. The horror of finding all her possessions strewn around the flat had been such a shock. She felt so violated. Someone—more than one some-one, it seemed—had broken in and rifled through her and her roommates' things. They had seen her photo with the girls at Stef's last birthday celebra-tion stuck on the kitchen door, which meant she might one day pass them in the street and they would know who she was but she would have no idea who they were. It was like being back on the university campus after that party. She didn't know who the enemy was. They had touched her cloth-ing, her underwear. Invaded her private sanctuary and now it was defiled, just as her body had been defiled all those years ago.

Cam kept glancing at her and gently squeezing and stroking her hand. It was enormously comfort-ing. Violet could see the concern, and the anger he was doing his best to suppress on her behalf. Was he thinking of what might have happened if she'd been in that flat alone? She was thinking about it and it was terrifying. How fortunate that he had walked her to the door. But then, of course he would do that. It was the type of man he was. Strong, capable, with old-fashioned values that resonated with hers.

His offer to have her stay with him at his house was perfectly reasonable given their friendship and yet…she wondered if he was entirely comfortable with it. Would it make it harder for him to keep things platonic between them?

Once they were back at his house, Cam carried her small bag of belongings—those she could stomach enough to bring with her—to one of the spare bedrooms. But at least her embroidery basket had been left intact. She was halfway through making a baby blanket for Lily's unborn baby and couldn't bear the thought of anyone destroying that.

'I'm only a door away over there.' Cam pointed to the master bedroom on the other side of the wide hallway. 'I'll leave my door open in case you need me during the night.'

I need you now.

'Thanks…for everything.'

He gave her one of those lopsided smiles of his that made her heart contract. 'You're welcome.'

Violet shifted her weight. 'Do you mind if I have a hot drink? I'm not sure I'm going to be able to sleep. Maybe a hot milk or something will help.'

'Of course.'

Violet followed him back down to the spacious kitchen and perched on one of the breakfast-bar stools while he went about preparing a hot chocolate for both of them. It was a strange feeling to be alone with him in his house, knowing she would be sleeping in one of his beds. Not *his* bed. He'd made that inordinately clear. But the possibility he could change his mind made her feel a thrill of excitement like someone had injected champagne bubbles into her bloodstream. She couldn't stop looking at his hands, couldn't stop imagining how they would feel touching her, stroking her. He had broad hands with long fingers with neat square nails. Capable hands. Careful hands. Hands that healed instead of hurt. Every time he touched her she felt her body glow with warmth. It was like she was coming out of cold storage. His touch awakened the sensuality that had been frozen by fear all those years ago.

He slid the hot chocolate towards her with a spoon and the sugar bowl. 'There you go.'

Violet took a restorative sip and observed him while he stirred his chocolate. He still had a twofold crease between his eyes as if his mind was still back at her flat thinking up a whole lot of nasty scenarios, similar to the ones she was trying her best not to think about. 'I'll only stay tonight,' she said into the silence. 'Once the girls and I tidy up, I'll go back.'

His frown wasn't letting up any. 'Is that such a good idea? What if you get broken into again? The security there is crap. You don't even have a security chain on the door. Your landlord should be ashamed of himself.'

'It's actually a woman.'

'Same goes.'

Violet cradled her drink between her hands, looking at him over the rim of her cup when she took another sip. He had abandoned his drink as if his mind was too preoccupied. There were lines of tension running down either side of his mouth. 'I know this must be awkward for you...having me here...' she said. 'You know, after our conversation earlier about...only kissing.'

His gaze went to her mouth as if he couldn't help himself. 'It's not awkward.' His voice came out so husky it sounded like it had been dragged along a rough surface.

'I could go to a hotel or stay with a—'

'No.' The word was delivered with such implacability it made Violet blink. 'You'll stay here as long as you need to.'

How about for the rest of my life? Violet took another sip of her chocolate before setting the mug down. She had to stop this ridiculous habit of imagining a future with him. She was being a silly romantic fool, conjuring up a happy ending because she was almost thirty and Cam was the first man to treat her the way she'd always longed to be treated.

It was her hormones…or something. 'I guess it kind of makes sense, me being here, since we're supposed to be engaged.'

'Yes, well, there's that, of course.'

Violet slipped off the stool and took her mug over to the sink, rinsing it first before putting it in the dishwasher. She turned and found Cam looking at her with a frowning expression. 'I'm…erm…going to bed now,' she said. 'Thanks again for everything.'

He gave her a semblance of a smile that softened the frown a smidgen. 'No problem. Hope you can get some sleep.'

Violet was about to turn for the door when, on an impulse she couldn't explain let alone stop, she stepped up to where Cam was standing and, rising on tiptoe, pressed a soft kiss to his stubble-roughened cheek. His hands went to her hips as if he too couldn't stop himself, drawing her that little bit closer so her body was flush against his. His eyes searched hers for a long moment before dipping to her mouth. 'We really shouldn't be doing this, Violet. It only makes things more—'

'More what?' Violet said, pressing herself closer, feeling the hardened ridge of him against her belly. 'Exciting?'

His hands tightened on her hips but, instead of drawing her closer, he put her from him, dropping his hold as if her body was scorching hot. His frown was severe but she got the feeling it was directed more at himself than at her.

'You're upset after the break-in,' he said. 'Your emotions are shot to pieces. It would be wrong of me to take advantage of you when you're feeling so vulnerable.'

Take advantage! Take advantage! Violet knew he was being the sensible and considerate man she knew him to be, but the fledging flirt in her felt hurt by his rejection. Why shouldn't they have a fling? It was the perfect chance for her to let go of her past and explore her sensuality without shame, without fear, with a man she not only trusted but admired and cared about. Why couldn't he see how much she needed him to help wipe away the past? 'I'm sorry for misreading the signals. Of course you wouldn't want to sleep with me. No one wants to sleep with me unless I'm coma-drunk. Why am I so hopeless at this?'

Cam took her by the shoulders this time, locking his gaze on hers. 'You're not hopeless at anything, sweetheart. You're a beautiful and talented young woman who deserves to be happy. I'm trying for damage control here. If we take this further, it will blur the boundaries. For both of us.'

Violet planted her hands on his chest, feeling the

thud-pitty-thud-pitty-thud of his heart beneath her palm. The battle was played out on his features: the push of pulsating desire and the pull away of his sense of duty. Push. Pull. Push. Pull. It was mirrored in the rhythm of a muscle flicking in his jaw. 'But you want me...don't you?' she said.

He brought her up against his body, pelvis to pelvis, his eyes holding hers. 'I want you, but—'

'Let's leave the "but" out of it,' Violet said. 'If I were anyone else, you'd have a fling with me, wouldn't you?'

He let out a short breath. 'You're not a fling type of girl so—'

'But what if I was? What if I wanted to have a fling with you because I'm so darn tired of being the girl without a date, the girl who hasn't had proper consensual sex? I'm sick of being that girl, Cam. I'm turning thirty in January. I want to find the courage to embrace my sexuality and who better with than you? Someone I trust and feel safe with.'

It was clear she had created a dilemma for him. His expression was a picture of conflict. His hands tightened on the tops of her shoulders, as if torn between wanting to bring her closer and pushing her away. 'I don't want to hurt you,' he said. 'That's the last thing I want.'

'How will you hurt me?' Violet asked. 'I'm not asking you to commit to anything permanent. I know that's not what you want and I'm fine with that.' *Not exactly true, but still.* 'We can have a fling for as long as our pretend engagement lasts. It will make it appear more authentic.'

He cupped her face with the broad span of his hand while his thumb stroked back and forth on her cheek. 'Looks like you've thought all of this through.'

'I have and it's what I want. It's what you want too, isn't it?'

His frown hadn't gone away but was pulling his brow into deep vertical lines between his eyes. 'What about your family?'

'What about them?' Violet said. 'They already think we're…together. Why shouldn't we therefore actually be together?'

'There's something a little off with your logic but I'm not sure what it is.'

'What's logical about lust?'

His frown was back. 'Is that all this is?'

'Of course.' Violet suspected she might have answered a little too quickly. 'I love you but I'm not *in* love with you.'

His eyes did that back and forth thing that made her feel as if he was looking for the truth behind the screen of her gaze. 'The thing is…good sex can make people fall in love with each other.'

Violet cocked her head. 'So, I'm presuming you've had plenty of good sex. Have you ever fallen in love?'

'No, but that doesn't—'

'Then what makes you think you will this time?'

He blinked as if he was confused about her line of argument. 'I'm not worried about me falling in love, I'm worried about you.'

Violet raised her brows. 'What makes you think you'll be immune to falling in love?'

He opened and closed his mouth, seemingly lost for an answer. 'Sex for me is a physical thing. I never allow my emotions to become involved.'

'Sounds like heaps of fun, just getting it on with someone's body without connecting with them on any other level.'

His brows snapped together and he dropped his hands from her hips. 'Damn it. It's not like that. At least I know their names and make sure they've given full and proper consent and are conscious.'

Violet wasn't going to apologise for her straight talking. In her opinion he was short-changing himself if he stuck to relationships that were based on mutual lust and nothing else. What about sharing someone's life with them? What about growing old together? What about being fully present in a relationship that made you grow as a person?

All the things she wished for but hadn't so far been able to find.

'You remind me of Fraser before he met Zoe. He was always saying he'd never fall in love. Look what happened to him. A chance meeting with Zoe and now he's married with twins and he couldn't be happier.'

Cam blew out a frustrated-sounding breath. 'It's different for your brother. He's had the great example your parents have set. He's had that since he was a baby—all of you have. I had a completely different example, one I wouldn't wish on a partner and certainly not on any children.'

Violet studied his tense expression, his even more rigidly set body and the way his eyes glittered with bitterness. And the way he had put some distance between their bodies as if he didn't trust himself not to reach for her. 'What exactly happened between your parents that you're so against marriage?'

It was a moment or two before he spoke. 'They only got married because my mother got pregnant with me. They were pressured into it by both of their families, although to be fair my mother was in love with my father, but unfortunately he didn't feel the same. It was a disaster from the word go. The earliest memories I have are of my parents fighting. They're the only memories I have, really.'

'But that doesn't mean you'd conduct a relationship like that,' Violet said. 'You're not that type of person.'

He gave a short laugh that had a note of cynicism to it. 'Thanks for the character reference but it won't be needed. I'm fine with how my life is now. I don't have to check in with anyone. I'm free to do what I want, when I want, with whomever I want.'

'As long as they're not married to your richest client or are your best friend's kid sister,' Violet said with a pointed look.

He pressed his lips together as if checking a retort. 'Violet…'

'It's fine.' Violet turned away with an airy wave of one hand. 'I get the message. You don't want to complicate things by sleeping with me. I'm not going to beg. I'll find someone else. After our engagement is over, of course.'

It was a great exit line.

And it would have been even better if she hadn't stumbled over the rug on her way out.

CHAPTER FIVE

CAM SWORE AND raked his hand through his hair until he thought he'd draw blood. Or make himself bald. What was he doing even *thinking* of taking her up on her offer of a fling? Violet was the last girl he should be thinking about. Tempted by. Lusting over. She was so innocent. So vulnerable. So adorable.

Yes, adorable, which was why he had to be sensible about this. She wasn't someone he could walk away from once the fling was over and never see or think of again. He would see her every time he was at a Drummond family gathering. He could avoid them, of course, but that would be punishing her family as well as himself.

Not that he didn't deserve to be punished for dragging her into this farce. If he hadn't asked her to that wretched dinner, none of this would have happened.

But if the dinner and the Christmas party tomorrow night weren't bad enough, now he had her under his roof in one of the spare bedrooms. Now he would spend the night, or however many nights she would be here, in a heightened state of arousal. Forget about cold showers, he would have to pump in water from the North Sea to deal with this level of attraction.

What was wrong with him?

Where was his self-control?

Why had he kissed her? That had been his first mistake. The second was to keep touching her. But he couldn't seem to keep his hands off her. As soon as she came within touching distance, he was at it again.

He had to stop thinking about making love to her. Stop picturing it. Stop aching for it. Just stop.

But truth was it was *all* Cam had been thinking about since running into Violet at that café. Which was damned annoying, as he'd never seen her that way before last Easter. For years she'd been one of the Drummond girls, just like Rose and Lily—a sister to him in every way other than blood. But it had all changed that last time he'd visited Drummond Brae. He could sense the exact moment when she turned her gaze on him. His body picked up her presence like a radar signal. His stomach rolled over and begged when she smiled at him. His skin tingled if she so much as brushed past him in a doorway. When his knees bumped hers under the table in the café he'd felt the shockwave travel all the way to his groin.

Even though she was safely in the spare room, he couldn't get her out of his mind. Her neat little ballerina-like figure, gorgeous brown eyes the colour of caramel, wavy chestnut hair that always smelled of flowers, a mouth that was shaped in a perfect Cupid's bow that drew his gaze more than he wanted it to. He had fantasies about that mouth. X-rated fantasies. Fantasies he shouldn't be having because she was like a sister to him.

Like hell she is.

Was that why he'd offered to bring her back here? Had some dark corner of his subconscious leapt at the opportunity to have her under his roof so he could take things to the next level? The level Violet wanted? The level that would change everything between them? Permanently. Irrevocably. How would he ever look at her in the future and not remember how her mouth felt under his? He was having enough trouble now getting it out of his mind. He could think of nothing else but how her mouth responded to his. How her lips had been as soft as down, her tongue both playful and shy. How her body felt when she'd brushed up against

him. How her dainty little curves made him want
to crush her to him so he could ease this relentless
ache of need. How he wanted to explore every inch
of her body and claim it, nurture it, release it from
its prison of fear.

But how could he do that, knowing she had so
much more invested in their relationship? She was
after the fairytale he was avoiding because loving
someone to that degree had the potential to ruin
lives. If—and it was a big if—he ever settled down
with a partner, he would go for a companionable relationship that was based on similar interests rather
than the fickleness of love that could fade after its
first flush of heat. His mother had paid the price—
was still paying it—for loving without caution. It
hadn't just ruined her life but that of several others along the way, as well. He didn't want that sort
of emotional carnage. He already had feelings for
Violet. Feelings that could slip into the danger zone
if he wasn't careful. Having her here under his roof
was only intensifying those feelings. The thought
of her being only a few doors away was a form of
torture. Making love with Violet would be exactly
that: making love. Encouraging love, feeding love,
nurturing it to grow and blossom. Sex was easy to
deal with if he kept his feelings out of it. But having sex with Violet would be all about feelings.

Emotions. Bonding. Commitment. All the things he shied away from because they had the potential to disrupt the neat and controlled order of his life.

He had to be strong. Determined. Resolute. Violet was looking for someone to give her heart to. She was vulnerable and it would be wrong of him to give her the impression an affair between them could go anywhere.

Why couldn't it?

Cam slapped the thought away like he was swatting away a fly. But it kept coming back, buzzing around the edges of his resolve, making him think of how it would be day after day, week after week, month after month, year after year with Violet in his life. Having her not just as a temporary houseguest but as a permanent partner. He wasn't so cynical that he couldn't see the benefits of a long-term marriage. He had only to look at Violet's parents to see how well a good marriage could work.

But how could he guarantee his would work? There were no guarantees, which was what scared him the most.

Violet didn't expect to sleep after the evening's disturbance. She thought she'd have nightmares about her flat being invaded but the only dreams she had were of Cam kissing her, touching her, making her feel things she'd never expected to feel. With time to reflect on it, she understood his caution about getting involved with her sexually. Of course it would be a risk. It would change everything about their relationship. Every single dynamic would be altered. You couldn't undo something like that. Every time she saw him at family gatherings in the future it would be there between them—their sensual history. He had only kissed her and held her and yet she was going to have a task ahead of her to forget about it. It was like his touch had seeped through every pore of her skin, tunnelling its way into her body so deep she instinctively knew she would never feel like that with anyone else. How could she? His touch was like a code breaker to her frozen sensuality. It unlocked the primal urges she had hidden away out of shame. He'd awoken those sleeping urges and now they were jumping up and down in her body like hyperactive kids on a trampoline.

Violet threw off the bedcovers and showered but when she looked at her overnight bag of belongings she'd hastily packed last night she knew she could never bring herself to touch them, let alone wear them. How could she know for sure if the intruders had touched them? What if she wore them and then out on the street the burglars recognised them as the ones they had rifled through last night? She had only the clothes she'd been wearing for the dinner last night. She didn't fancy putting them on again after her shower and, besides, the velvet cocktail dress was hardly Saturday morning wear. It was way too dressed up. If she went out in that get-up, she would look like she had been out all night. She rinsed out her knickers and dried them with the hairdryer she found in one of the drawers in the bathroom. There was a plush bathrobe hanging on the back of the bathroom door so she slipped it on over her underwear.

Cam was in the kitchen pouring cereal into a bowl when she came in. He looked up and Violet saw the way his eyes automatically scanned her body as if he was imagining what she looked like underneath the bathrobe. He cleared his throat and turned back to his cereal, making rather a business of sealing the inside packet and folding down the flaps on top of the box. 'Sleep okay?'

'Not bad…'

He took a spoon out of one of the drawers and then turned and opened the fridge for the milk. Violet drank in the image of him dressed in dark blue jeans and a black finely woven cashmere sweater with a white T-shirt underneath. There should be a law against a man looking so good in casual clothes.

The denim hugged his trim and toned buttocks; the close-fitting sweater showcased the superb musculature of his upper body. His hair was still damp from a shower and it looked like his fingers had been its most recent combing tool, for she could see the finger-spaced grooves between the dark brown strands.

'What would you like for breakfast?' he said, turning from the fridge. 'I'm afraid I can't match your mother's famous breakfast spreads but I can do cereal, toast and fruit and yoghurt.'

'Sounds lovely.' Violet perched on the stool opposite him. 'Can I ask a favour?'

His gaze met hers. 'Look, we had this discussion last night and the answer is—'

'It's not about…that.' Violet captured her lip between her teeth. Did he have to rub it in? So he didn't want to sleep with her. Fine. She wasn't going to drag him kicking and screaming to the nearest bedroom. 'It's about my clothes. I need to get new ones. I can't bear wearing any of mine from the flat, not even the ones I brought with me, and I don't want to wear my cocktail dress because I'll look like I've been out all night.'

A frown pulled at his forehead. 'You want me to go…shopping for you?'

Did he have to make it sound like she'd asked

him to dance naked in Trafalgar Square? 'I'll give you my credit card. I just need some basics and then I can do the rest myself once you bring those couple of things back.'

He blew out a breath and reached for a pen and a slip of paper, pushing it across the bench. 'Write me a list.'

Cam had never shopped for women's clothing before. Who knew there was so much to choose from? But choosing a pair of jeans and a warm sweater wasn't too much of a problem. The problem was he kept looking at the lingerie section and imagining Violet in the sexy little lacy numbers. He had to walk out before he was tempted to buy her the black lace teddy with the hot pink feathers. Or the red corset one with black silk lacing. Once he'd completed his mission, he was making his way back to his house when he walked past a jewellery store. He'd walked past that store hundreds, if not thousands, of times and never looked in the window, let alone gone in. But for some reason he found himself pushing the door open, going inside and standing next to the ring counter.

It's just a prop.

Violet's office party was tonight and what sort of cheap fiancé would he look if he hadn't bought her a decent ring? No need to mortgage the house on a diamond but that one at the back there looked perfect for Violet's hand. He didn't have too much trouble guessing her ring size; he had thought of her hands—holding them, feeling them on his skin—enough times to know the exact dimensions. Actually, he knew pretty much the exact dimensions of her whole body. They were imprinted on his brain and kept him awake at night.

Cam paid for the ring, placed it in his pocket and walked out of the store. Just as he was about to turn the corner for home, he got a call from Fraser. He couldn't avoid the conversation any longer, but something about lying to his best mate didn't sit too comfortably. 'Hey, sorry I haven't returned your calls,' he said. 'Things have been happening so fast I—'

Fraser gave a light laugh. 'You don't have to apologise to me, buddy. I saw the way you were looking at Vivi at Easter. Is that why you skived off to Greece? So you wouldn't be tempted to act on it?'

Maybe it had been, now that he thought about it. Cam often had to travel abroad at short notice in order to meet with a client, but the chance to go to Greece for a few months had been exactly the escape hatch he'd needed. He'd felt the need to clear his head, to get some perspective, to have a little talk to himself about stepping over boundaries that couldn't be undone. But the whole time he'd been away, Violet had been on his mind. 'Yeah, well, now that you mention it.'

'Great news, man,' Fraser said. 'Couldn't be more delighted. Zoe reckons this is going to be the best Christmas ever. Did you hear about Grandad? Talk about a turnaround. He's so excited for your wedding.'

The wedding that wasn't going to happen... Cam sidestepped the thought like someone avoiding a puddle. 'Yeah, your mum told me. It's great he's feeling better.'

'So when's the big day? Am I going to be best man? No pressure or anything.'

Cam affected a light laugh. 'I've got to get my father's fifth wedding out of the way first. We'll set a date after that.'

'What's your new stepmother like?'

'Don't ask.'

'Like that, huh?'

'Yep,' Cam said. 'Like that.'

Violet looked around Cam's house while he was out. It was a stunningly beautiful home with gorgeous touches everywhere but on closer inspection it didn't have a personal touch, nothing to hint at the private life of its only occupant. There were no family photos or childhood memorabilia. Unlike her family home in Scotland, where her mother had framed and documented and scrapbooked each of her children's milestones, Cam's house was bare of anything to do with his childhood. There were no photos of him with his parents. None of him as a child. It was as if he didn't want to be reminded of that part of his life.

Violet turned from looking at one of the paintings on the wall in the study when Cam came in carrying shopping bags. 'You've been ages,' she said. 'Was it frightfully busy? The shops can be a nightmare at this time of year. I shouldn't have asked you. I'm sorry but I—'

'It was fine.' He handed her the bags. 'You'd better check I've got the right size.'

Violet took the bags and set them on the cedar desk. She took out the tissue-wrapped sweater and held it against her body. It was the most gorgeous baby-blue cashmere and felt soft as a cloud. The other wrapped parcel was a pair of jeans. But there was another tiny parcel at the bottom of the second shopping bag. Her heart gave a stumble when she picked it up and saw the high-end jewellery store label on the ribbon that was tied in a neat bow on top. 'What's this?'

'An engagement ring.'

Violet's eyes rounded. Her heart pounded. Her hopes sounded. *Did this mean...? Was he...?* 'You bought a ring? For me?'

His expression was as blank as his house was of his past. 'It's just for show. I figured everyone would be asking to see it at your office party tonight.'

Violet carefully unpeeled the ribbon, her heart feeling like a hummingbird was trapped in one of its chambers. She opened the velvet box to find a beautiful diamond in a classic setting in a white gold ring. It was more than beautiful—it was perfect. How had he known she wasn't the big flashy diamond sort? She took it out of the box and pushed it onto her ring finger. It winked up at her as if in conspiracy. *I might be just a prop but don't I look fabulous on your hand?* She looked up at Cam's unreadable expression. 'It's gorgeous. But I'll give it back after Christmas, okay?'

'No.' There was a note of implacability to his tone. 'I want you to keep it. Think of it as a gift for your help with the Nicolaides contract.'

Violet held up her hand, looking at the light dancing off the diamond. She didn't like to think it might be the only engagement ring she ever got. She lowered her hand and looked at him again. 'It's very generous of you, Cam. It's beautiful. I couldn't have chosen better myself. Thank you.'

'No problem.'

Violet gathered up her new clothes and the packaging. 'I'm going to get dressed and head out to replenish my wardrobe. What are your plans?'

'Work.'

'On the weekend?'

He gave her a *that's how it is* look. 'I'll catch up with you later this evening. What time is your office party?'

'Eight.'

'I'll be back in time to take you. Make yourself at home.' He reached past her to open the drawer of the desk and took out a key on a security remote. He handed it to her. 'Here's the key to the house.'

Violet took the key and a rush of heat coursed from her fingers to her core when her hand came into contact with his. He must have felt it too for his gaze meshed with hers in a sizzling tether that made her wonder if he was only going to work to remove himself from the temptation of spending time with her. Doing…things. Wicked things. Things that made her blood heat and her stomach do cartwheels of excitement. 'Cam?' Her voice came out croaky and soft.

His eyes went to her mouth and she saw the way

his throat moved up and down over a tight swallow. 'Don't make this any harder than it already is.' His tone was two parts gravel, one part honey, and one part man on the edge of control.

With courage she had no idea she possessed, Violet moved closer, planting her hands on his chest, bringing her hips in contact with his. 'Don't I get to kiss you for buying me such a gorgeous ring?'

His eyes darkened until it was impossible to tell where his pupils began and ended. His body stirred against hers, the swell of his erection calling out to her. Desire burned through every lonely corridor of her body, every network of nerves, every circuit of her blood. She became aware of her breasts pushed up against the fabric of her bathrobe, the nipples already tight, her flesh aching for human touch—Cam's touch. Her courage increased with every pound of his heart she could feel thundering under her palm.

His head came down at the same time she stepped up on tiptoe, their mouths meeting in the middle in an explosion of lust that sent a shockwave through Violet's body. It sent it through Cam's, too, for he grabbed her by the hips and pulled her hard against him, smothering a groan as his mouth plundered hers.

His tongue didn't ask for entry but demanded it,

tangling with hers in a sexy combat that mimicked the intimacy both of them craved. This wasn't a chaste kiss between old friends. This was a kiss of urgency, of frustration, of long-built-up needs that could wait no longer for satiation.

Cam's mouth continued its thrilling exploration of hers while his hands slipped beneath the opening of her bathrobe, exposing her breasts. Violet shivered as the feel of his hand shaping her, cupping her, caressing her threatened to heat her blood to boiling. She'd had no idea her breasts were that sensitive. No idea how wonderful it felt to have a man's hand cradle her shape while his thumb moved back and forth across her nipple.

But it wasn't enough. Her body wanted more. More contact, more friction, more of the sensual heat his body promised. She pushed her lower body against his, relishing the delicious thrill it gave her to feel the potency of his arousal. She had done that to him. Her body stirred his as his stirred hers. It was a combustible energy neither of them could deny nor ignore any longer.

'This is madness,' Cam said just above her mouth.

Violet didn't give him a chance to pull away any further. She pressed closer, stroking her tongue over his lips, the top one and then the lower one, a shiver coursing through her when he gave another rough groan and covered her mouth in a fiery kiss. His hands gripped her by the hips, holding her to his rigid heat, the contact making Violet's inner core tingle and tighten with anticipation. How had she survived so long without this magical energy rushing through her body? Cam's touch made every nerve in her body cry out for more.

He pulled his mouth away, his breathing a little unsteady. 'Not here, not like this.'

Violet kept her arms around his waist, reluctant to give him the opportunity to break the intimate contact. 'Don't say you don't want me because I know you do.'

He gave her a rueful look. 'Not much chance of hiding it, is there? But I want you to be comfortable and making love on a desk or the floor is not my idea of comfortable.'

Before Violet could say anything, he scooped her up in his arms. She gave a startled gasp and held on, secretly delighted he was taking charge like a romantic hero out of an old black and white movie.

They came to his bedroom door and he shouldered it open and carried her to the end of the bed, lowering her to the floor, but not before trailing her body down the length of his, leaving her in no doubt of his erotic intentions. He pressed another lingering kiss to her lips, exploring the depths of her mouth with a beguiling mix of gentleness and urgency. Sensations rippled through her body in tiny waves, making her skin sensitive to his touch like he had cast a sensual spell on her. But then he had. From the moment he had walked into that café, she had been under the heady spell of sexual attraction.

Violet pulled up his sweater and T-shirt so she could glide her hands over his naked skin. Warm, hard male flesh met the skin of her palms; a light smattering of masculine hair grazed her fingertips, the scent of his cologne teased her nostrils. She explored the tiny pebbles of his nipples, and then the flat plane of his stomach with its washboard ridges that marked him as man who enjoyed hard physical exercise.

Cam untied the waist strap of her bathrobe and sent his hands on their own sensual journey. Violet shuddered when his hands glided around her ribcage, not quite touching her breasts but close enough for her to feel she would die if he didn't. He brought his mouth to the upper curve of her right breast. He didn't seem in a hurry, but maybe he was giving her time to get used to this level of intimacy. He brushed his thumb over her nipple, a back and forth movement that made her body contract with want.

Rather than undress her any further, he set to work on his own clothes, taking each item off while his gaze was trained on hers.

Finally, he was in nothing but black underpants, and then and only then did he remove her bathrobe. Violet's belly did a somersault an Olympic gymnast would have been proud of when she saw the way his eyes feasted on her breasts. He cupped them in his hands with exquisite care, rolling his thumb over each nipple before lowering his mouth to subject her to an intimate torture that made her senses spin in dizzying delight.

He lifted his mouth off her breast and, kneeling in front of her, continued to kiss his way from her sternum to her belly button. Violet sucked in a breath, her hands on his shoulders, not sure she could handle what he was planning.

'Relax, sweetheart.'

Easy for you to say. Violet held her breath while he peeled away her knickers. The warmth of his breath on her intimate flesh made her spine weaken as if someone had unbolted her vertebrae. His mouth came to her softly, a light as air touch that made her knees tremble. He gently parted her, stroking her with his tongue, the sensation so powerful she pulled away. 'I—I can't…'

His hands were gentle but firm on her hips. 'Yes, you can. Don't be frightened of it. Trust me.'

Violet glanced down at him worshipping her body, his touch so tender, so respectful it made her see her body differently, not as something to be ashamed of and hidden away, but as something that was not only beautiful and capable of receiving pleasure, but also of giving it too. The rhythmic strokes of his tongue sent a torrent of tingles through her body, concentrating on that one point— the heart of her femininity. The tension grew to a crescendo until she was finally catapulted into a vortex that scattered her thoughts until all she could do was feel. Feel the power of an orgasm that swept through her like a hot wave, rolling through every inch of her flesh, trickling over every nerve ending, sending showers of goose bumps over her body, leaving no part of her immune. She was limbless, dazed, out of her mind as the aftershocks pulsed through her.

Cam brought his mouth back up over her stomach and ribcage, then her breasts, leaving a blistering trail of kisses on her tingling skin. He stood upright, drawing her closer, his mouth settling back on hers in a mind-altering kiss, the eroticism of it heightened by the fact she could taste her own essence on his lips and tongue.

Violet had thought herself too shy to draw his briefs from his body but somehow her hands reached for the elastic edge of the waistband and slid them away from his body. She took him into her hand—hot, hard, and quintessentially male. She stroked him with experimental caresses, her fingers drawing down from the base to the head and back again. It was so empowering to be an active part of a sexual encounter. The deep guttural noises he made added to her sense of agency. She was doing this to him. She was the one he wanted. She was the one exciting him, pushing him to the limit of control.

Cam gently moved her hand away and guided her to the mattress behind her, coming down over her in a tangle of limbs, balancing his weight on his arms so as not to crush her. 'Comfortable?'

'Yes.' Violet was surprised she was capable of thought, let alone speech. The way he made her feel, so safe, so treasured, made the shame she had carried for so long slip further out of reach, like an old garment stuffed at the back of the wardrobe. It was still there but she could no longer see it.

Cam stroked her face with his fingertip, his eyes dark and lustrous. 'We don't have to go any further if you're not ready.'

I'm ready! I'm ready! Violet touched the flat of her palm to his stubbly jaw, looking into his eyes without reserve. 'I want you inside me.'

A flash of delight went through his gaze. 'I won't rush you and you can stop me at any point.'

He reached for a condom in the bedside drawer and deftly applied it before coming back to her. The choreography of their bodies aligning themselves for that ultimate physical connection was simple and yet complex. It was like learning the steps to a dance, one leg this way, the other that, her breasts pressing against the wall of his chest, her arms winding around his body to anchor herself. He gently probed her entrance, allowing her time to adjust to him just…being there. She felt the weight and heft of him waiting there but it wasn't threatening in any way.

He slowly entered her, waiting for her to relax before going any further. Violet welcomed him inside her body with soft little gasps as the sensation of him stretching her, filling her, tantalising her gained momentum. He began a slow rhythm that sent shivers of delight through her body, the friction of male against female making her aware of her body in a way she had never been before. Nerves she hadn't known existed were firing up. Muscles that had been inactive for most of her life were now being activated in a deeply pleasurable workout that had one sure goal. She could feel that goal dangling just out of reach, the thrill of her flesh building and building but unable to go any further. It was a frustrating ache, a restless urging for more. But, as if Cam could read her silent pleas for release, he brought his hand down between their bodies and sought the heart of her arousal. The stroking of his fingers against her tipped her into a free fall of spinning, whirling, dizzying sensations. They ricocheted through her in giant shudders, making her lose her grasp on conscious thought. She was in the middle of a vortex, vivid colours bursting like thousands of tiny fireworks behind her squeezed-shut eyelids.

Then the slow wash of a wave of lassitude… She was drifting, drifting, drifting…

But then she became aware of the increasing pace of Cam's thrusts as his own release powered down on him. She experienced every second of it through the sensitised walls of her body, his tension building to a final crucial point before he pitched forwards against her, his deep primal cry making something in her belly shiver like a light wind whispering over the surface of a lake.

Violet lay in his embrace, her fingertips moving up and down his spine while his breathing gradually slowed. She couldn't find the words to express what her body had just experienced. She felt reborn. As if the old her had been sloughed away like a tired skin. Her new skin felt alive, energised, and sensitive to every movement of Cam's breathing as his chest rose and fell against hers.

Should she say something? What? *How was it for you?* That seemed a little trite and clichéd somehow. How many times had he lain here like this with other women? How many other women? He might not be the fastest living playboy on the planet but he wasn't without a sex life. He just kept it a little more private than other men in his position. How many women had lain here in his arms and felt the same as her? Was what she had experienced with him run-of-the-mill sex? Or was it different? More special? More intense?

Violet knew she was being a fool for allowing her feelings to get involved. But this was Cam. Not just some hot guy she happened to fancy. Cam was a friend. Someone she had known for years and years and always admired.

They had stepped into new territory and it felt… weird, but not horribly weird. Nicely weird. Excitingly weird. Would he make love to her again? How soon? Would he get so hooked on having sex with her he would extend their 'engagement'? What if he fell in love with her? What if he decided marriage and kids wasn't such a bad idea? What if—?

Cam dealt with disposing of the condom and then looked down at her with a soft smile that made his eyes seem even darker. 'Hey.'

Violet hoped he wasn't as good at reading her mind as he was at reading her body. Her thoughts were running like ticker tape in her head. *Please fall in love with me. Please.*

'Hey...'

He brushed some stray strands of hair back from her face, his smile fading as a frowning concern took up residence instead. 'Did I hurt you?'

Violet had trouble speaking for the sudden lump in her throat. 'N-not at all.'

He picked up another strand of hair and gently anchored it behind her ear, holding her gaze with his. 'Sure?'

How was she supposed to keep her feelings out of this when he looked at her like that? When his hands touched her as if she were something so eminently precious to him he would rather die than hurt her? 'I'm sure.'

He leaned down to press a soft kiss to her mouth. 'You were wonderful.'

Violet traced the line of his mouth with her fingertip. 'This won't...change things between us, will it? I mean, no matter what happens, we'll always be friends, won't we?'

A flicker of something moved through his gaze like a passing thought leaving a shadow in its wake. 'Of course we will.' He took her hand and quickly kissed the ends of her fingertips before releasing it. 'Nothing will ever change that.'

Violet wasn't so sure. What if she couldn't cope with going back to normal? He might be able to go back to relating to her as he had always done, but she wasn't confident she would be able to do the same to him. How could she look at him and not think of how his mouth felt against her own? How could she not think of how his hands had stroked her most intimate flesh? How could she not think of how his body had awakened hers and made her feel things she hadn't thought were possible to feel?

Not just physical things, but emotional things.

Things that might not be so easily set aside once their fling was over.

CHAPTER SIX

CAM WAITED WHILE Violet had a shower and got changed. He would have joined her but he was conscious of allowing her time to recover. God, *he* needed time to recover. So much for keeping his distance. So much for his self-control. Where had that gone? He hadn't been able to resist the temptation of making love to her. So apparently they were having a fling. It didn't feel like any fling he'd ever had before. He had never known a partner the way he knew Violet. Her trust in him had heightened the experience. Every touch, every kiss, every stroke, every whimper or gasp of hers had made his pleasure intensify. It was like having sex for the first time but not in a clumsy, awkward way, but in a magical, mutually satisfying way that left his body humming like a plucked string.

Somehow the thought of spending the afternoon working didn't hold its usual appeal. Even a yuletide cynic like him had to agree there was no greater place to be before Christmas than in London. He wasn't much of a shopper but Violet needed a new wardrobe and he would rather spend the time with her than chained to his desk.

Violet came down the stairs wearing the jeans and baby-blue sweater he'd bought her. Cam had trouble keeping his hands to himself. He ached to slide his hands under the sweater and cradle the perfection of her breasts. To feel those pink nipples embed themselves into his palm. To feel her body quake with pleasure when he touched her.

She smiled at him shyly, her cheeks going a faint shade of pink as if she too were recalling their earlier intimacy. 'I thought you were going to work?'

Cam shrugged. 'It can wait.' He took her hand and brought it up to his mouth. 'I probably should warn you I'm not the world's best shopper but I'm pretty handy with carrying bags.'

Her eyes shone as if the thought of him accompanying her pleased her as much as it pleased him. 'Are you sure you're not too busy? I know how much men loathe shopping. Dad and Fraser are such pains when we try to get them through a department store door.'

Cam looped her arm through his. 'I have a vested interest in this expedition. I have to make sure Cinderella is dressed appropriately for the ball tonight.'

A flicker of worry passed through her gaze. 'I never know what to wear to the office party. There's a theme this year… *A Star-Struck Christmas*. Last year it was *White Christmas*. The year before it was *Christmas on the Titanic*.'

'You could turn up in a bin liner and still outshine everyone else.'

Her smile made something in his chest slip sideways. 'I really appreciate you coming with me. I can't tell you how much I hate going alone.'

Cam bent down to press a kiss to her forehead. 'You're not alone this year. You're with me.'

Cam wasn't much of a party animal but even he had to admit Violet's firm put on a Christmas extravaganza that was impossible not to enjoy. It occupied the ballroom of one of London's premier hotels and the decorations alone would have funded a developing nation for a year. Giant green and gold and red Christmas bells hung from silken threads just above head height. Great swathes of tinsel adorned the walls. A fresh Christmas tree was positioned to one side of the room, covered with baubles that looked like they had been dipped in gold. Maybe they had. There was an angel on the top whose white gown glittered with Swarovski crystals. The music was lively and fun. The food was fabulous. The champagne was top-shelf and free flowing.

Or maybe he was having a good time because he was with the most beautiful girl at the party. The shimmery dress he'd helped Violet choose skimmed her delicate curves so lovingly his hands twitched in jealousy. The heels she was wearing put his mind straight in the gutter. He couldn't stop imagining her wearing nothing but those glossy black spikes and a sexy come-and-get-me smile.

Cam had been ruminating all afternoon over whether he had done the right thing in making love to Violet. Who was he kidding? He was *still* ruminating. It was like a loop going round and round in his head. *What have I done?*

It was fine to put it down to hormones, but he wasn't some immature teenager who didn't know the meaning of the word self-control. He was a fully grown adult and yet he hadn't been able to walk away.

Had he done the wrong thing?

His body said *Yes*.

His mind said *Yes, but*.

The *buts* were always going to be the kicker. Violet wasn't like any other casual lover he'd met. She'd been in his life for what seemed like for ever. He'd seen her grow from a gangly and shy teenage girl to a beautiful young woman. She was still shy but some of that reserve had eased away when they'd made love. Sharing that experience with her, being the one to guide her through her first experience of pleasure with a partner had been special. More than special. A sacred privilege he would remember for the rest of his life. Her trust in him had touched him, honoured him, and made him feel more of a man than he had ever felt before.

But...

How could he give her what she wanted when it was the opposite of what he wanted right now? Violet came from a family where marriage was a tradition that was celebrated and treasured and believed in. She wanted the fairytale her parents and siblings had.

It wasn't that Cam was so cynical he didn't think marriage could work. It did work. It worked brilliantly, as Margie and Gavin Drummond demonstrated and their parents before them. But Cam's parents' example had made him see the other side of the order of service: the stonewalling, the bitter fights, the disharmony, the petty paybacks, the affairs and then the divorce lawyers, not to mention years of estrangement where the very mention of the other person's name would bring on an explosive fit of temper.

While Cam didn't think he was the type of person to walk out on a commitment as important as marriage, how could he be sure life wouldn't throw up something that would challenge the standards he upheld? The promises people made so earnestly in church didn't always ring with the same conviction when life tossed in a curve ball or two.

It was all well and good to be confident he would stand by his commitment, but it wasn't just about his commitment. The other person would have to be equally committed. How could he be sure Violet, as gorgeous and sweet as she was, would feel the same about him in ten weeks, let alone ten years or five times that? Watching his parents go through their acrimonious divorce when he was a young child had made him wary about rushing into the institution.

He had never had any reason to question his decision before now. It had always seemed the safest way to handle his relationships—being open and honest about what he could and couldn't give. Yes, some lovers might have been disappointed there was no promise of a future. But at least he hadn't misled them.

But sleeping with Violet had changed things.

Changed *him*. Made him more aware of the things he would be missing out on rather than the things he was avoiding. Things like walking into a party hand in hand, knowing he was going to leave with that hand still in his. Knowing the smile she turned his way was for him and no one else. Recognising the secret look she gave him that told him she was remembering every second of his lovemaking and she couldn't wait to experience it again. Feeling the frisson of awareness when she brushed against him, how his body was so finely tuned to hers he could sense her presence even when she was metres away.

Had he ever felt like that with anyone else? No. Never. Which wasn't to say he wouldn't with someone else…someone other than Violet. His gut swerved at the thought of making love to someone else. He couldn't imagine it. Couldn't even picture it. Couldn't think of a single person who would excite him the way she excited him.

It will pass. It always does.

Lust for him was a candle not a coal ember. It would flare for a time and then snuff out. Sometimes gradually, sometimes overnight.

But when he looked at Violet, he couldn't imagine his desire for her ever fading. Because his desire for her wasn't just physical. There was another quality to it, a quality he had never felt with anyone else. When he'd made love to her it had felt like an act of worship rather than just sex. Her response to him had been a gift rather than a given. The fact she trusted him enough to feel able to express herself sexually was the biggest compliment—and turn on—he had ever experienced.

But...

How was he going to explain the end of their 'engagement' to her family? How was he going to go back to being just friends? How would he be able to look at her and not remember the way her mouth had felt when she'd opened it for him that first time? How her shy little tongue had tangled with his until his blood had pounded so hard he'd thought his veins would explode? How would he be able to be in the same room as her without wanting to draw her into his arms? To feel her slim body press against his need until he was crazy with it?

Maybe he was crazy. Maybe that was the problem. Making love to her was the craziest thing he'd done in a long time.

But...

He wanted to make love to her again. And again and again.

God help him.

* * *

Violet was coming back from a trip to the ladies'
room when she was intercepted by three of her
workmates, including Lorna.

'Congratulations, Violet,' Lorna said, eyeing her
engagement ring. 'Gracious me, that man of yours
was quick off the mark.' Her gaze flicked to Violet's
abdomen. 'You're not pregnant, are you?'

If there was one time in her life Violet wished
she didn't have the propensity to blush, this was it.
Could Lorna tell the engagement wasn't real? After
all, Violet hadn't mentioned anything about dating
anyone, not that she talked about her private life
that much at work. But women working together for
a long time tended to pick up on those things. Besides, conversations around the water cooler tended
to show how boring her life was compared to everyone else's. 'No, not yet but it's definitely on the
to-do list.' *Why did you say that?*

Lorna's smile didn't involve her eyes. 'When's
the big day?'

'Erm…we haven't decided on a date yet,' Violet
said. 'But some time next year.' *I wish.*

'So how did he propose?'

Violet wished she'd talked this through a little
more with Cam. They hadn't firmed up any de-

tails of their story apart from the fact—which was indeed a fact—they had met via her older brother. How would Cam propose if he were going to ask her to marry him? He wasn't the bells and whistles type. There wouldn't be any skywritten proposals or football-stadium audiences while he got down on bended knee. That was the sort of thing his father did, even on one memorable occasion making the evening news. Cam would choose somewhere quiet and romantic and tell her he loved her and wanted to spend the rest of his life with her. Her heart squeezed. *If only!* 'It was really romantic and—'

'Ah, here's Prince Charming himself,' Lorna said as Cam approached. 'Violet's been telling me how you proposed.'

Cam's smile never faltered but Violet knew him well enough to notice the flicker of tension he was trying to disguise near his mouth. He slipped an arm around Violet's waist and drew her close against him. 'Have you, darling?'

Violet's smile had a hint of *help me* about it. 'Yes, I was saying it was terribly romantic…with all the roses and…stuff.'

'What colour?' Lorna asked.

'White,' Violet said.

'Red,' Cam said at exactly the same time.

Lorna's artfully groomed brows rose ever so

slightly. But then she smiled and winked at Cam. 'You have good taste. Violet's a lucky girl to land a man who knows his way around a diamond dealer.'

'She deserves the very best,' Cam said.

'Yes, well, she's waited long enough for it,' Lorna said and with a fingertip wave moved on to return to the party.

Violet released a long jagged breath. 'She suspects something. I know she does. We should've talked about the proposal.' She spun around so her back was to the party room. 'I feel such an idiot. And, for the record, I hate red roses.'

'I'll make a note of it.'

Violet searched his expression but he had his blank-wall mask on. 'So how would you propose if you were going to?'

His brows moved together over his eyes. 'Is that a trick question?'

'No, it's a serious one,' Violet said. 'If, and I know it's a very big "if", but if you were to ask someone to marry you how would you go about it?'

Cam glanced about him. 'Is this the right venue to talk about this?'

Violet wasn't going to risk being cornered by another workmate for details of their engagement. Nothing would out a charade faster than someone cottoning on to a clash of accounts of an event from witnesses. 'We're out of earshot out here. Come on, tell me. What would you do?'

He blew out a short breath. 'I'd make sure I knew what the girl would like.'

'Like what colour roses?'

He gave her a droll look. 'What have you got against red roses?'

Violet gave a lip shrug. 'I don't know... I guess because they're so obvious.'

'Right, then I'd make sure we were alone because I don't believe in putting a woman under pressure from an audience.'

'Like your father did with wife number three?'

'Number two and three.' Cam's eyes gave a half roll.

'So no TV cameras and news crews?'

'Absolutely not.'

Violet looked back at the party in the next room. 'We should probably go and mingle...'

'What's your dream proposal?' Cam asked.

She met his gaze but there was nothing to suggest he was asking the question for any other reason than mild interest. 'I know this sounds a bit silly and ridiculously sentimental, but I've always wanted to be proposed to at Drummond Brae. Ever since I was a little girl, I dreamed of standing by the loch near the forest with the house in the distance and my lover going down on bended knee, just as my father did with my mum and my grandfather did with my grandmother.'

'Your would-be fiancé would have to have a meteorological degree to predict the best time to do it.' Cam's tone was dry. 'Nothing too romantic about being proposed to in sleet or snow.'

Violet's smile was wistful. 'If I was in love I probably wouldn't even notice.'

Half an hour later, Violet turned back to Cam after listening to a boring anecdote from one of her coworkers who'd had one too many drinks. Cam was staring into space and had a frown etched on his brow. 'Are you okay?' she said, touching him on the arm.

He blinked as if she'd startled him but then he seemed to gather himself and smiled down at her. 'Sure.' He slipped an arm around her waist and drew her closer. 'Did I tell you you're the most beautiful woman in the room?'

Violet could feel a blush staining her cheeks. Did he mean it or was he just saying it in case other people were listening? She felt beautiful when she was with him. What woman wouldn't when he looked at her like that? As if he was remembering every moment of making love to her. The glint in his dark eyes saying he couldn't wait to do it again. 'Don't you feel a little…compromised?'

'In what way?'

She glanced around at the partying crowd before returning her gaze to his, saying sotto voce, 'You know…pretending. Lying all the time.'

He picked up her left hand and pressed a kiss to the diamond while his eyes stayed focused on hers. 'I'm not pretending to want you. I do and badly. How long do we have to stay?'

Violet's inner core tingled in anticipation. 'Not much longer. Maybe five, ten minutes?'

He dropped a kiss to her forehead. 'I'm going to get a mineral water. Want one?'

'Yes, please.'

'Hey, Violet.' Kenneth from Corporate Finance came up behind her and placed a heavy hand on her shoulder. 'Come and dance with me.'

Violet rolled her eyes. She went through the same routine with Kenneth every year at the Christmas party. He always had too much to drink and always asked her to dance. But, while she didn't want to encourage him in any way, she knew Christmas for him was a difficult time. His wife had left him just before Christmas a few years ago and he hadn't coped well with the divorce. Violet turned and gently extricated herself from his beefy paw. 'Not tonight, thanks. I'm with my…fiancé.'

Kenneth looked at her myopically, swaying on his feet like his body couldn't decide whether to stand or fall. 'Yeah, I heard about that. Congrats and all that. When's the big day?'

'We haven't got around to settling on that just yet.'

He grabbed her left hand and held it up to the light. 'Nice one. Must've cost a packet.'

Violet didn't care for the clammy heat of his hand against hers. But neither did she want to make a scene. The firm had strict guidelines on sexual harassment in the workplace but she felt sorry for Kenneth and knew he would be mortified by his behaviour if he were sober. 'Please let me go, Kenneth.'

He lurched forwards. 'How about a Christmas kiss?'

'How about you get your hands off my fiancée?' Cam said in a tone as cold as steel.

Kenneth turned around and almost toppled over and had to grab hold of the Christmas tree next to him. Violet watched in horror as the tree with all its tinsel and baubles came crashing down, the snow-white angel on the top landing with a thud at Violet's feet, her porcelain skull shattering.

The room was suddenly skin-crawlingly quiet.

But then Kenneth dropped to his knees and picked up the broken angel and held it against his heaving chest. His sobs were quiet sobs. The worst sort of sobs because what they lacked in volume they made up for in silent anguish.

Violet went down beside him and placed a comforting hand on his shoulder. 'It's all right, Kenneth. No one cares about the tree. Do you want us to give you a lift home?'

To her surprise Cam bent down on Kenneth's other side and place his hand on the man's other shoulder. 'Hey, buddy. Let's get you home, okay?'

Kenneth's eyes were streaming tears like someone had turned on a tap inside him. He was still clutching the angel, his hands shaking so much the tiny bits of glitter and crystals from her dress were falling like silver snow. 'She's having a baby... My ex, Jane, is having the baby we were supposed to h-have...'

Violet had trouble keeping her own tears in check. How gut-wrenchingly sad it must be for poor Kenneth to hear his ex-wife was moving on with her life when clearly he hadn't stopped loving her. She exchanged an agonised glance with Cam before leaning in to one-arm-hug Kenneth. She didn't bother trying to search for a platitude.

What could she say to help him recover from a broken heart? It was obvious the poor man wasn't over his divorce. He was lonely and desperately sad, and being at a party where everyone was having fun with their partners was ripping that wound open all over again.

After a while, the music restarted and the crowd went on partying. Cam helped Kenneth to his feet while some other men helped put the tree back up.

Violet collected their coats and followed Cam and Kenneth out to the foyer of the hotel where the party was being held. She waited with Kenneth while Cam brought the car to the door and within a few minutes they were on their way to the address Kenneth gave her.

He lived in a nice house in Kensington, not unlike Cam's house, but Violet couldn't help thinking how terribly painful it must be for Kenneth to go home to that empty shell where love had once dwelled, where plans had been made and dreams dreamt.

Once they were sure Kenneth was settled inside, Cam led Violet back to his car. 'Sad.'

'I know...'

'Did you see all the photos of his ex everywhere?' Cam said. 'The place is like a shrine to her. He needs to find a way to move on.'

'I know, but it must be so hard for him at Christmas especially.'

He gave her hand a light squeeze. 'Sorry for being a jerk about him touching you.'

'That's okay, you weren't to know.' She let out a sigh. 'It must be terrible for him, seeing everyone else having a good time while he comes back here to what? An empty house.'

'Does he have any other family? Parents? Siblings?'

'I don't know…but even if he did, wouldn't being with them just remind him of what he's lost? It's hard when you're the only one without a partner.' Violet knew that better than anyone.

Cam nodded grimly. 'Yeah, well, divorce is harder on some people than others.'

Violet glanced at him. 'Your mother took it hard?'

The line around his mouth tightened. 'I was six years old when they finally split up. A week or two after my father moved out to live with his new partner, I came downstairs one morning to find her unconscious on the sofa with an empty bottle of pills and an empty wine bottle beside her. I rang Emergency and thankfully they arrived in time to save her.'

No wonder he was so nervous about commitment. Seeing the devastation of a breakup at close quarters and at such a tender age would have been nothing short of terrifying. 'That must have been so scary for you as a little kid.'

'Yeah, it was.' He waited a beat before continuing. 'Every time I went back to boarding school after the holidays I was worried sick about her. But she started seeing another guy, more to send a message to my father than out of genuine love. It was a payback relationship—one of many.'

'No wonder you break out in a rash every time someone mentions the word marriage,' Violet said.

'Divorce is the word I hate more. But you can never know if it's going to happen or not. No one can guarantee their relationship will last.'

Violet wanted to disagree but deep down she knew what he said was true. There were no guarantees. Life could change in a heartbeat and love could be taken away by disease or death or divorce. Just because you were in love didn't mean the other person would remain committed. She knew many women and men who'd been devastated by their partners straying. But she believed in love and commitment and knew she would do her best when she fell in love to nurture that love and keep it healthy and sustained.

What do you mean—when you fall in love? Haven't you already?

Violet waited until they'd gone a few blocks before speaking again. 'Cam? I have to do something about my flat tomorrow. I really should have done something about it today but I couldn't bring myself to face it. But I can't leave that mess for the girls to clean up on their own.'

'Do you have to go back there?'

Violet glanced at him again. 'What do you mean? It's where I live.'

'You could live somewhere else. Somewhere safer, more secure.'

'Yeah.' Violet sighed. 'Somewhere heaps more expensive too.'

There was a silence broken only by the swishing of the windscreen wipers going back and forth.

'You could stay with me for as long as you like,' Cam said. 'Until you find somewhere more suitable, I mean. There's no rush.'

Violet wondered what was behind the invitation. Was it solely out of consideration for her safety or was he thinking about extending their relationship until who knew when? 'That's a very generous offer but what if you want to start seeing someone else after we break up after Christmas? Could be awkward.'

'Everything about this situation is awkward.'

Violet looked at the tight set of his features. 'Are you regretting…what happened this morning?'

He relaxed his expression and reached across the gear console and captured her hand, bringing it over to rest on top of his thigh. 'No. Maybe I should, but I don't.'

'I don't regret it either.'

His eyes met hers when he parked the car. 'Your family is going to be hurt when we…end this.'

Why had he hesitated over the word 'end'? Who would end it? Would it be a mutual decision or would he suddenly announce it was over?

'Yes, I feel bad about that. But at least it's not for long,' Violet said. 'Once Christmas is over we'll say we made a mistake…or something and go back to normal.'

He studied her for a long moment. 'Will you be okay with that?'

Violet gave him a super-confident smile. 'Of course. Why wouldn't I be? It's what we agreed on. A short-term fling to get me back on my dating feet.'

His expression clouded. 'You have to be careful when you're dating guys these days. You can't go out with just anyone. It's not safe when there are so many creeps on the prowl. And don't do online dating. Some of those guys lie about their backgrounds. Anyone can use a false identity. You could end up with someone with a criminal past.'

Violet wondered if he was cautioning her out of concern or jealousy or both. 'You sound like you don't want me to date anyone else.'

He paused before responding. 'I care about you, Violet, that's all. I don't want you to become a crime statistic.'

'I'm sure I'll manage to meet and fall in love with some perfectly lovely guy, just like my sisters have done,' Violet said. 'I'm just taking a little longer than they did to get around to it.'

He opened his car door and came around to hers but, instead of tension, this time there was a self-deprecating tilt to his mouth. 'Sorry about the lecture.'

Violet smiled and patted his hand where it was resting on the top of the doorframe. 'You can lecture me but only if I can lecture you right on back. Deal?'

He bent down to press a kiss to the end of her nose. 'Deal.'

CHAPTER SEVEN

CAM WOKE FROM a fitful sleep to find the space next to him in the bed was empty. He sat bolt upright, his chest seizing with panic. Where was Violet? When he'd drifted asleep she had been lying in his arms.

Calm down, man. She's probably gone to the bathroom.

He threw off the bedcovers and, snatching up a towel, wrapped it around his hips and padded through his house, checking each room and bathroom upstairs but there was no sign of her.

'Violet?' His voice rang out hollowly. His blood chugged through his veins like chunks of ice. His skin shrank away from his skeleton. He was annoyed at his reaction. What did it say about him? That he was so hooked on her he couldn't let her out of his sight? Ridiculous. She had a right to move about the house without asking permission first. Maybe she'd had trouble sleeping with him in the bed beside her. After all, she'd never been in a proper relationship before. Sharing a bed with someone took some getting used to, which was why he generally avoided it.

'Violet?'

Where could she be? Had she gone outside? He tugged the curtains aside but the back garden was as quiet and deserted as a graveyard. It was three in the morning and it was bitterly cold. Had she gone back to her flat? No. She wouldn't go there without backup. He flung open the sitting room door, then the study.

All empty.

'Are you looking for me?' Violet appeared like a ghost in the doorway of the study.

Relief flooded through Cam like the shot of a potent drug. 'Where were you?'

Her eyes did a double blink at the edginess of his tone. 'I was reading in the breakfast room.'

Cam frowned so hard his forehead pinched. 'Reading?'

Her tongue snaked out and left a layer of moisture over her lips. 'I was…having trouble sleeping. I didn't want to disturb you. You seemed restless enough without me putting on the light and rustling pages.'

Cam forked a hand through his already tousled

hair. 'You should've woken me if I was disturbing you. Was I snoring?'

'No, you were just…restless like you were having a bad dream or something.'

He had been having a bad dream. It was coming back to him now in vivid detail. He had been alone in a run-down castle. The drawbridge was up and there was no way in or out. Loneliness crept out from every dark corner, prodding him with tomb-cold fingers. The yawning emptiness he felt was what he had seen on Kenneth's face when they'd returned him to his home last night: the absence of hope, the presence of despair, the bitter sting of regret.

But it was a dream. It didn't mean anything. It was just his mind making up a narrative while his body rested. It didn't mean he was worried about ending up alone in a castle with nothing but cobwebs and shadows to keep him company. It didn't mean he was subconsciously regretting his stance on marriage and commitment. It meant he was dog-tired and working too hard. That was what it meant. That. Was. All. 'Sorry for wrecking your beauty sleep. Next time just give me a jab in the ribs, okay?'

Violet's shy smile tugged like strings stitched on to his heart. 'It was probably my fault more than yours. I've never spent the night with anyone before.'

Of course she hadn't. She might have felt all sorts of uncomfortable about sharing the night with him in his bed. Cam put his hands on her hips and brought her closer. 'I'm not much of a sleep-over person myself.'

A flicker of concern appeared in her gaze. 'Oh... well, then, I can sleep in one of the spare rooms if you'd—'

'No.' Cam brought his mouth down to within an inch of hers. 'I like having you in my bed.' *More than I want to admit.*

Her hint of vanilla danced over his mouth. 'I like it too.'

Cam covered her mouth with his, a shockwave of need rushing through him as her lips opened beneath his. He moved his lips against hers, a gentle massage to prove to himself he could control his response to her. But within seconds the heat got to him, the flicker of her tongue against his lower lip unravelling his self-control like a dropped ball of string. He splayed his fingers through her silky hair, holding her face so he could deepen the kiss. She gave a soft whimper of approval that made his body shudder in delight.

Her body pressed against his, her breasts free

behind the bathrobe she was wearing. Knowing she was naked underneath that robe made him wild with need. He untied the waistband, still with his mouth on hers, letting it fall to her feet. He glided his hands over her breasts and then he brought his mouth to each one in turn, caressing the erect pink nipples with his tongue, gently taking them between his teeth in a soft nibble. She smelt of flowers and sleep and sex and he couldn't get enough of her.

He brought his mouth back to hers, his hands holding her by the hips so she could feel what she was doing to him. The ache of need pounded through his body, the primal need to mate driving every other thought out of his brain.

He should have taken her upstairs to the bed but he wanted her now. *Now.*

The hunger was in time with his racing pulse. He wanted her on the floor. On the desk. On the sofa. Wherever he could have her. He dragged his mouth off hers. 'I want you here. Now.'

Violet's eyes shone with excitement. She didn't say anything but her actions spoke for her. She stroked her hands down his chest to his abdomen, deftly unhooking the towel from around his waist and taking him in her hands. Her touch wreaked havoc on his control. Red-hot pleasure shot through his body, luring him to the abyss where the dark magic of oblivion beckoned.

Cam had to stop her from taking him over the edge. He drew her hand away and guided her to the floor. He kissed his way down from her breasts to her belly, lingering over her mound, ramping up her anticipation for what was to come. She squirmed and whimpered when he claimed his prize, her body bucking within seconds of his tongue moving against her. Her cries of pleasure made him want her all the more. Her passion was so unfettered, so unrestrained it made him wonder if she would find the same freedom to express her sexuality with someone else.

Someone else...

Cam tried to push the thought aside but it was impossible. It was ugly, grotesque thinking of Violet with some other guy. Someone who might not appreciate her sensitivity and shyness. Someone who might pressure her into doing things she wasn't comfortable with doing. Someone who wouldn't protect her at all times and in all places.

That's rich coming from the guy who hasn't got a condom handy.

Violet must have sensed Cam's shift in mood for she propped herself up on her elbows to look at him. 'Is something wrong? Did I do something wrong?'

Cam took her by the hand and helped her to stand. 'It's not you, sweetheart. It's me.' He handed her the bathrobe before picking up his towel and hitching it around his waist. 'I didn't bring a condom with me.'

'Oh...'

'Unlike other men, I don't have them strategically planted in every room of the house.' *But maybe I should.*

Her lips flickered with a smile. 'That's kind of nice to know...'

'I'm selective when it comes to choosing partners.' He only ever chose women he knew he wouldn't fall in love with: safe, no-strings women who were out for a bit of fun and a tearless goodbye at the end of it. Women who didn't look at him with big soulful brown eyes and pretend they didn't feel things they clearly felt.

How was he going to end this?

Do you even want to?

Cam played with the idea of extending their affair. But how long was too long and how short was too short? Either way, it still left him with the task of facing her family and saying the happy ever after they were hanging out for wasn't going to happen.

And that wasn't even the half of it. What about what Violet felt? No matter how much she said she was only after a short fling, he knew her well enough to know she was only saying that to please him. Would it be fair to continue this, knowing she was probably falling in love with him? God knew he was having enough trouble keeping his own feelings in check. Feelings he couldn't explain. Feelings that crept up on him at odd moments, like when Violet looked at him a certain way, or when she smiled, or when she touched him and it sent a lightning zap of electricity through him. Feelings he couldn't dismiss because Violet wasn't a temporary fixture in his life.

The longer he continued their affair, the harder it would be to end it. He knew it and yet…and yet… he couldn't bring himself to do it. Not until after Christmas. Grandad Archie surely deserved to have his last Christmas wish?

Violet made a business of tying the bathrobe back around her waist. 'I suppose you're careful to choose partners you're not likely to fall in love with.'

'It's easier that way.' Maybe that was why he never felt fully satisfied after an encounter even when the sex was good. Something always felt a little off centre. Out of balance, like only wearing one shoe. He never let a relationship drag on for too long. A month or two maximum. It made him look like a bit of a player but that was the price he was prepared to pay for his freedom.

Violet gave him a smile that didn't quite make the grade. 'Lucky me.'

Cam frowned. 'Hey, I didn't mean I chose you for that reason. You're different, you know you are.'

'Not different enough that you'll fall in love with me.'

'Violet—'

She held up her hand. 'It's okay, I don't need the lecture.'

Cam took her by the shoulders again. 'Are you saying you're in love with me? Is that what you're saying?'

Her eyes did everything they could to avoid his. 'No, I'm not saying that.' Her voice was hardly more than a thread of sound.

Cam tipped up her chin, locking her gaze with his. 'This is all I can give you. You have to accept it, Violet. Even if we continued our relationship past Christmas, it would still come down to this. I'm not going to get married to you or to anyone just now.'

Her shoulders went down on a sigh. 'I know. I'm being silly. Sorry.'

He brought her head against his chest, stroking her silky hair with his hand. 'You're not being silly.

You're being normal. I'm the one with the commitment issues, not you.'

Her arms snaked around his waist. 'Can we go back to bed now?'

Cam lifted her in his arms. 'What a great idea.'

Violet had arranged with Cam to take her back to her flat on Sunday afternoon to help Amy and Stef with the clean-up, but while she was getting breakfast ready while Cam checked some emails, Amy phoned.

'You're not going to believe this,' Amy said. 'But last night old Mr Yates in twenty-five was smoking in bed and started a fire—'

'Is he all right?' Violet asked.

'Just a bit of smoke inhalation but both our flats are uninhabitable from the water damage,' Amy said. 'The landlady is furious and poor Mr Yates won't want to face her in a hurry.'

'So what will we do?' Violet asked. 'Are we expected to clean it up or will a professional cleaning service do that?'

'Cleaning service,' Amy said. 'I'm not going in there until the building's secure. The ceiling might come down or something. Stef's going to move back in with her mum and I'm going to move in with Heath. We've talked about moving in together for ages so this nails it. What about you? Will you stay with Cam now that you're officially engaged?'

'I... Yes, that's what I'll do,' Violet said. What else could she say? *No, Cam doesn't want to live with anyone*?

Cam came in at that point and smiled. It never failed to make her shiver when he looked at her like that. He stroked a hand down her back while he reached past her to take a mug out of the cupboard next to her. It was the lightest touch but it sent a tremor of longing through her flesh until her legs threatened to buckle.

Violet said goodbye to Amy and put her phone on the bench. 'I have a slight problem...'

'What's wrong?'

She explained about the fire and the water damage. 'So, I have to find somewhere else to live.'

It was hard to read his expression beyond the concern it showed while she had related the events of last night's fire. He turned to one side to take out a tea bag from a box inside the pantry. 'You can stay here as long as you need to. I told you that the other day.'

'Yes, but—'

'It's fine, Violet, really.'

'No, it's not fine,' Violet said. 'A couple of weeks is okay, but any longer than that and things will get complicated.' *More complicated than they already were.*

'What if I help you find a place?'

'You don't have to do that.'

'I'd like to,' he said. 'It'll mean I can give the security a once-over.'

Violet gave him a grateful smile. 'That would be great, thanks.' She waited a beat before adding, 'What's happening with the contract with Nicolaides? Is it secure yet?'

'Not yet.' Cam pulled out one of the breakfast-bar stools. 'I have some drawings to finalise. Sophia keeps altering the design, I suspect because she wants to drag out the process.'

'Has she sent you any more texts?'

'A couple.'

Jealousy surged in Violet's gut. 'When's she going to get the message? What is wrong with her?'

He gave a loose shrug. 'Some women don't know the meaning of the word no.'

Violet would have to learn it herself and in a hurry. 'I think it's disgusting how she openly lusts over you while her husband is watching. Why does he put up with it?'

'He's too frightened to lose her,' Cam said. 'She's twenty years younger than him. And she brings a lot of money to the relationship. Her father left her his empire. It's worth a lot of money.'

'I wouldn't care how much money someone had. If I couldn't trust them, then that would be it. Goodbye. Have a good life.'

He stroked a fingertip down her cheek, his smile gently teasing. 'If you think Sophia's bad, wait till you meet my father's fiancée.'

Violet frowned. 'You want me to meet her?'

'My dad's organised drinks on Wednesday night,' Cam said. 'If you'd rather not go, then—'

'No, it's okay. Of course I'll go. You went to my boring old office party, the least I can do is come with you for drinks with your father.'

Cam's father, Ross, had arranged to meet them at a boutique hotel in the centre of London. Violet hadn't met Ross McKinnon before but she had seen photos of him in the press. He was not quite as tall as Cam and his figure showed signs of the overly indulgent life he led. His features had none of the sharply chiselled definition of Cam's, and while he still had a full head of thick hair, it was liberally sprinkled with grey. His eyes, however, were the same dark blue but without the healthy clarity of Cam's. And they had a tendency to wander to Violet's breasts with rather annoying frequency.

'So this is the girl who's stolen my son's hard heart,' Ross said. 'Congratulations and welcome to the family.'

'Thank you,' Violet said.

Ross pushed his fiancée forward. 'This is Tatiana, my wife as of next weekend. We should have made it a double wedding, eh, Cameron?'

Cam looked like he was in some sort of gastric pain. 'Wouldn't want to steal your thunder.'

Violet took the young woman's hand and smiled. 'Lovely to meet you.'

Tatiana's smile came with a don't-mess-with-me warning. 'Likewise.'

Cam was doing his best to be polite but Violet could tell he was uncomfortable being around his father and new partner. Ross dominated the conversation with occasional interjections from Tatiana, followed by numerous public displays of affection that made Violet feel she was on the set of a B-grade porn movie. Clearly she wasn't the only one as several heads kept turning at the bar, followed by snickers.

Ross showed no interest in Cam's life. It shocked Violet that his father could sit for an hour and a half in his son's company and not once ask a single question about his work or anything to do with his private life. It made her feel sad for Cam to have had such a selfish parent who acted like a narcissistic teenager instead of an adult.

Violet was relieved when Cam got to his feet and said they had to leave.

'But we haven't told you what we've got planned for the honeymoon,' Ross said.

'Isn't that supposed to be bad luck?' Cam said with a pointed look.

Ross's face darkened. 'You can't help yourself, can you? But Tatiana is the one. I know it as sure as I'm standing here.'

'Good for you.' Cam's tone had a hint of cynicism to it and Violet wondered how many times he had heard exactly the same thing from his father. Ross was the sort of man who treated women as trophies to be draped on his arm and summarily dismissed when they ceased to pander to his bloated ego.

Violet quickly offered her hand to Ross and Tatiana. 'It was lovely to meet you. I hope the wedding goes well.'

Ross frowned. 'But aren't you coming with Cameron?'

Violet realised her gaffe too late. 'Erm…yes, of course, if that's what you'd like.'

'You're part of the family now,' Ross said. 'We'd be delighted to have you share in our special day, wouldn't we, babe?'

Tatiana's smile was cool. 'But of course. I'll aim the bouquet in your direction, shall I?'

Violet's smile felt like it was stitched in place. 'That'd be great.'

Cam took her by the hand and led her out of the hotel. 'I did warn you.'

'How on earth do you stand him?' Violet said. 'He's impossibly self-centred. He didn't ask you a single thing about your work or anything to do with you. It was all about him. How amazing he is and how successful and rich. And Tatiana looks like she's young enough to be his daughter. What on earth does she see in him?'

'He paid for her boob job.'

Violet rolled her eyes. She walked a few more paces with him before adding, 'I'm sorry about the wedding gaffe. I didn't think. Do you think they suspected anything was amiss?'

'Probably not,' Cam said. 'They're too focused on themselves.'

'Poor you,' Violet said.

He gave a soft smile. 'You want to grab a bite to eat before we go home?'

Go home. How...permanent and cosy that sounded. 'Sure. Where did you have in mind?'

'Somewhere on the other side of the city so

there's no chance my father and Tatiana will chance upon us.'

Violet gave him a sympathetic look. 'I swear I am never going to complain about my family ever again.'

'There's no such thing as a perfect family,' he said. 'But I have to admit yours comes pretty close.'

Violet adored her family. They were supportive and loving and always there for her. But the pressure to live up to the standards her parents had modelled for her always made her feel as if she wasn't quite good enough, that she would never be able to do as brilliant a job as they had of finding love and keeping it. It was one of the reasons she had never told her mother or her sisters about what had happened at that party. Although she knew they would be nothing but supportive and concerned, she'd always worried they would see her differently...as damaged in some way.

'I know, but it's hard to live up to, you know? What if I don't find someone as perfect as my dad is for my mum? They're such a great team. I don't want to settle for less but I'm worried I might miss out. I want to have kids. That makes me feel under even more pressure. It's all right for guys; you can have kids when you're ninety. It's different for women.'

'If it's going to happen it'll happen,' he said. 'You can't force these things.'

'Easy for you to say. You have a queue of women waiting to hook up with you.'

He gave her hand a tiny squeeze. 'I'm only interested in one woman at the moment.'

At the moment.

How could she forget the clock ticking on their relationship? It was front and centre in her mind. Each day that passed was another day closer to when they would go back to being friends. Friends *without* benefits. It would be torture to be around Cam without being able to touch him, to kiss him, to wrap her arms around him and feel his body stir against her. It would be torture to see him date other women, knowing they were experiencing the explosive passion and pleasure of being in his arms.

What if she never found someone as perfect for her as Cam? What if she ended up alone and had to be satisfied with being an aunty or godmother instead of the mother she longed to be? She had been embroidering baby clothes since she was a teenager. She'd made them for her sisters and brother's wife Zoe each time they were expecting but she had her own private stash of clothes. It was her version of a hope chest. Every time she looked at those little vests and booties and bibs she felt an ache of longing. But it wasn't just about having a baby, she realised with a jolt. She wanted to have *Cam's* baby. She couldn't think of anything she wanted more than to be with him, not just for Christmas but for ever.

After dinner they walked hand in hand through the Christmas wonderland of London's streets. Violet had always loved Christmas in her adopted city but being with Cam made the lights seem all the brighter, the colours all the more vivid, the hype of the festive season all the more exciting. When they walked past the Somerset House ice-skating rink, Cam stopped and looked down at her with a twinkling look. 'Fancy a quick twirl to work off dinner?'

Violet looked at the gloriously lit rink with the beautifully decorated Christmas tree at one end. She had skated there a couple of times with Stef and Amy but she'd felt awkward because they had brought their boyfriends. The boys had offered to partner her but she'd felt so uncomfortable she'd pretended to have a sore ankle rather than take them up on their offer. 'I'm not very good at it...' she said. 'And I'm not wearing the right clothes.'

'Excuses, excuses,' Cam said. 'It won't take long to go home and change.'

Within a little while they were back at the rink

dressed in jeans and jackets and hats and gloves. Violet felt like a foal on stilts until Cam took her by the hand and led her around until she felt more secure. He looked like he'd been skating all his life, his balance and agility making her attempts look rather paltry in comparison.

'You're doing great,' he said, wrapping one arm around her waist. 'Let's do a complete circuit. Ready?'

Violet leaned into his body and went with him in graceful sweeps and swishes that made the cold air rush past her face. It was exhilarating to be moving so quickly and with his steady support she gained more and more confidence, even letting go of his hand at one point to do a twirl in front of him.

Cam took her hand again, smiling broadly. 'What did I tell you? You're a natural.'

'Only with you.' *And not just with skating.* How would she ever make love with someone else and feel the same level of pleasure? It didn't seem possible. It wasn't possible because there was no way she could ever feel the same about someone else.

Once they had given back their skates, they walked to the London Eye, where Cam paid for them to go on to look at the Christmas lights all over London. Violet had been on the giant Ferris wheel a couple of times but it was so much more special doing it with Cam. The city was a massive grid of twinkling lights, a wonderland of festive cheer that made all the children and most of the adults on board exclaim with wonder.

Violet turned in the circle of Cam's arms to smile at him. 'It's amazing, isn't it? It makes me get all excited about Christmas when usually I'm dreading it.'

A slight frown appeared on his brow. 'Why do you dread it? I thought you loved spending Christmas with your family.'

Violet shifted her gaze to look at the fairyland below. 'I do love it…mostly, it's just I'm always the odd one out. The one without a partner. Apart from Grandad, of course.'

His hand stroked the small of her back. 'You won't be without a partner this year.'

But what about next year? Violet had to press her lips together to stop from saying it out loud. Once Christmas was over so too would their relationship come to an end. All the colour and sparkle and excitement and joy would be snuffed out, just like someone turning off the Christmas lights.

'No one knows what the next year will bring,' Cam said as if he had read her thoughts. 'You could be married and pregnant by then.'

I wish…but only if it were to you. 'I can't see that

happening.' Violet waited a moment before adding, 'Would you come to my wedding if I were to get married?'

Something flashed across his face as if pain had gripped him somewhere deep inside his body. 'Would I be invited?' His tone was light, almost teasing, but she could sense an undercurrent of something else. Something darker. Brooding.

'Of course,' Violet said. 'You're part of the family. It wouldn't be a Drummond wedding if you weren't there.'

'As long as you don't ask me to be the best man,' he said with a grim look. 'My father's asked me to be his and that'll be four times in a row.'

'Wow, you must be an expert at best man speeches by now.'

'Yeah, well, I hope this is the last time but I seriously doubt it.'

Violet thought of her parents and how loving and committed they were to each other and had been from the moment they'd met. They renewed their wedding vows every ten years and went back to the same cottage on the Isle of Skye where they'd spent their honeymoon on each and every anniversary. How had Cam dealt with his father's casual approach to marriage? Ross McKinnon changed wives faster than a sports car changed gears. How embarrassing it must be for Cam to have to go through yet another wedding ceremony knowing it would probably end in divorce. 'Maybe this time will be different,' she said. 'Maybe your dad is really in love this time.'

Cam's expression was a picture of cynicism. 'He doesn't know the meaning of the word.'

CHAPTER EIGHT

THE NEXT DAY Cam came home from work with the news that his contract with Nick Nicolaides had been signed that afternoon.

'Let's go out to celebrate.' He bent down to kiss Violet on the mouth. 'How was your day?'

Violet looped her arms around his neck. 'My day was fine. You must be feeling enormously relieved. Was Sophia there at the meeting?'

'Yes, but she was surprisingly subdued,' he said. 'I think she might've been feeling unwell or something. She got up to leave a couple of times and came back in looking a bit green about the gills. Too much to drink the night before, probably.'

Violet's brow furrowed. 'Could she be pregnant?'

He gave a light shrug. 'I wouldn't know, although, now that I think of it, Nick was looking pretty pleased with himself. But I thought that was because we finally finalised the contract.'

'Maybe being pregnant will help her settle down with Nick instead of eyeing up other men all the time,' Violet said.

Cam stepped away to shrug off his coat, laying it over the back of a chair. His expression had a cloaked look about it, shadowed and closed off. 'A Band-Aid baby is never a good idea.'

Violet knew he was bitter about his parents and the way they had handled his arrival in the world. Did he blame himself for how things had turned out? How could he think it was his fault? His parents were both selfish individuals who ran away from problems when things got the slightest bit difficult. They moved from relationship to relationship, collecting collateral damage along the way. How many lives had each of them ruined so far? And it was likely to continue with Ross McKinnon's next marriage. No wonder Cam wanted no part of the type of marriage modelled by his parents. It was nothing short of farcical. 'True,' she said. 'But a baby doesn't ask to be born and once it arrives it deserves to be treasured and loved unconditionally.'

A frown pulled at Cam's forehead. 'We haven't discussed this before but are you taking any form of oral contraception?'

Violet felt her cheeks heat up. It was something

she had thought about doing but she hadn't got around to making an appointment with her doctor to get a prescription. There hadn't seemed much point when she wasn't dating regularly. But now... now it was imperative she kept from getting pregnant. The last thing Cam would want was a baby to complicate things further, even though she could think of nothing more wonderful than falling pregnant with his child. 'I'm not but I'm sure it won't be a problem—'

'Condoms are not one hundred per cent reliable,' he said, still frowning.

Violet felt intimidated by his steely glare. Why did he have to make her feel as if she was deliberately trying to get pregnant? There were worse things in the world than falling pregnant by the man you loved. Much worse things. Like not getting pregnant at all. Ever. 'I'm not pregnant, Cam, so you can relax, okay?'

A muscle tapped in his cheek. 'I'm sorry but this is a big issue for me. I don't want any mishaps we can't walk away from.'

Violet cast him a speaking look. 'You'd be the one walking away, not me.'

His frown deepened. 'Is that what you think? Really? Then you're wrong. I would do whatever I could to support you and the baby.'

'But you wouldn't marry me.' It was a statement, not a question.

For once his eyes had trouble meeting hers. 'Not under those circumstances. It wouldn't be fair to the child.'

Violet moved away to fold the tea towels she had taken out of the clothes dryer earlier. 'This is a pointless discussion because I'm not pregnant.' *And I wouldn't marry you if I were because you don't love me the way I long to be loved.*

'When will you know for sure?'

'Christmas Day or thereabouts.'

A silence ticked past.

Cam picked up his jacket and slung it over his arm. 'I'm going to have a shower.' He paused for a beat to rub at his temple as if he was fighting a tension headache. 'By the way, thanks for doing the washing. You didn't need to do that. My housekeeper will be back after Christmas.'

'I had to do some of my own so it was no bother.'

He gave her a tired-looking smile. 'Thanks. You're a darling.'

Violet disguised a despondent sigh. *But not* your *darling.*

Cam couldn't take his eyes off Violet all evening. They had gone to one of his favourite haunts, a piano bar where the music was reflective and calming. She was wearing a new emerald-green dress that made her creamy skin glow and her brown eyes pop. Her hair was loose about her shoulders, falling in soft fragrant waves he couldn't wait to go home and bury his head in.

But there was something about her expression that made him realise he had touched on a sensitive subject earlier. Babies. Of course he'd had to mention contraception. He had the conversation with every partner. It was the responsible thing to do. A baby—*he*—had ruined his mother's life. It had changed the direction of her life, her career plans, her happiness—everything. A thing she unfortunately reminded him of when she was feeling particularly down about yet another broken relationship.

But Violet wanted a baby. And why wouldn't she? Her siblings were growing their young families and she was the only one left single.

Not quite single...

Cam picked up his glass and took a measured sip. Weird how he felt...so committed and yet this was supposed to be temporary.

Violet raised her glass, a smile curving her lips. 'Congratulations, Cam. I'm so happy for you about the contract.'

'Thanks.' He couldn't think of a single person he would rather celebrate his contract with. It wasn't as if either of his parents were interested, and while Fraser was always thrilled for him when he won an award or landed a big contract, it wasn't the same as having someone who wanted your success more than their own.

'About our conversation earlier…' Cam said.

'It's fine, Cam,' Violet said. 'I understand completely.'

'It's tough on women when they get pregnant. I realise that,' Cam said. 'Even today when there is so much more support around. It's a life-changing decision to keep a baby.'

'Did your mother ever consider…?' Violet seemed unable to complete the sentence.

'Yes and no.' Cam leaned forward to put his glass down. 'She kept me because by doing so she thought she'd be able to keep my father. But when that turned sour, she decided she wished she'd got rid of me so she could have continued her studies.'

Violet frowned. 'She told you that?'

He gave an I'm-over-it shrug. 'Once or twice.'

'But that's awful! No child, no matter how young or old, should hear something like that from a parent.'

'Yes, well, I was an eight-pound spanner in the

works for my mother's aspirations. But I blame my father for not supporting her. He got on with his career without a thought about hers.' Cam passed Violet the bowl of nuts before he was tempted to scoff the lot. 'Have you ever thought of going back and finishing your degree?'

Her mouth froze over her bite into a Brazil nut. She took it away from her mouth and placed it on the tiny, square Christmas-themed napkin on the table between them. 'No... I'm not interested in studying now.'

'But you were doing English Literature and History, weren't you?' Cam said. 'Didn't you always want to be a teacher?'

Her eyes fell away from his and she dusted the salt off her fingers with another napkin. 'I'm not cut out for teaching. I'd get too flustered with having to handle difficult kids, not to mention their parents. I'm happy where I'm working.'

'Are you?'

Her eyes slowly met his. 'No, not really, but I'm good at it.'

'Just because you're good at something doesn't mean you should spend your life doing it if it bores you,' Cam said. 'Why don't you study online? Even if you don't teach, it will give you some closure.'

Violet pushed her glass away even though she

had only taken a couple of sips. Her cheeks were a bright shade of pink and her mouth was pinched around the edges. 'Can we talk about something else?'

Cam leaned forwards, resting his forearms on his thighs. 'Hey, don't go all prickly on me. I'm just trying to help you sort out your life.'

Her eyes flashed with uncharacteristic heat. 'I don't need my life sorting out. My life is just fine, thank you very much. Anyway, you need to sort out your own life.'

He sat back and picked up his glass. 'There's nothing wrong with my life.'

Her chin came up. 'So says the man who only dates women who won't connect with him emotionally. What's that about, Cam? What's so terrifying about feeling something for someone?'

Losing them.

Like his mother had lost his father and gone on to lose every other partner since in a pattern she couldn't break because the one person she had loved the most hadn't wanted her any more.

Cam didn't want to be that person. The person left behind. The person who gave everything to the relationship only to have it thrown away like trash when someone else more exciting came along.

He was the one in control in his relationships.

He started one when he wanted one.

He left when it was time to go.

'We're not talking about me,' Cam said. 'We're talking about you. About how you're letting a bad thing that happened to you rob you of reaching your full potential.'

'But isn't that what you're doing? You're letting your parents' horrible divorce rob you of the chance of long-term happiness because you're worried you might not be able to hang on to the one you love.'

So what if he was? He was fine with that. It wasn't as if he was in love with anyone anyway. *You sure about that?* Cam blinked the thought away. Of course he loved Violet. He had always loved her. But it didn't mean he was *in* love with her.

Yes, you are.

No, I'm not.

The battle went back and forth in his head like two boxing opponents trying to get the upper hand. He was confusing lust with love. The sex was great—better than great—the best he'd ever had. But it didn't mean he wanted to tie himself down to domesticity. He was a free agent. Marriage and kids were not on his radar. Violet was born to be a mother. Any fool could see that. She went dewy-eyed at the sight of a baby. She embroidered baby clothes for a hobby, for goodness' sake.

Even puppies and kittens turned her to mush. She had planned her wedding day since she was a kid. He had seen photos and home videos of her and her sisters playing weddings. Violet had looked adorable wearing her mother's veil and high heels when she was barely four years old.

How could he ask her to sacrifice that dream for him?

Violet began chewing at her lip. 'Are you angry at me?'

Cam reached across and took her hand. 'No, of course not.' He gave her hand a gentle squeeze. 'Would you like to dance?'

Her eyes lit up. 'You want to dance?'

'Sure, why not?' He drew her to her feet. 'I might not be too flash with a Highland fling but I can do a mean waltz or samba.'

Her arms linked around his neck, bringing her lower body close to the need already stirring there. 'I didn't mean to lecture you, Cam. I hate it when people do that to me.'

Cam pressed a soft kiss to her mouth. 'I'm sorry too.'

Violet had always been a bit of a wallflower at her home town's country dances. She stood at the back of the room and silently envied her parents, who twirled about the dance floor as if they were one person, not two. But somehow in Cam's arms she found her dancing feet and moved about the floor while the piano played a heartstring-pulling ballad as if she was born to it. His arms supported her, his body guided her and his smile delighted her. 'If you tell your brother about this I'll have to kill you,' Cam said.

Violet laughed. 'Someone should be videoing this because no one's going to believe I've got through three songs without doing you an injur— Oops! Spoke too soon.' She glanced down at his feet. 'Did I hurt you?'

'Not a bit.' He guided her around the other way, drawing her even closer to his body.

Violet loved the feel of his arms around her, but the slow rhythm of the haunting melody of lost love reminded her of the time in the not too distant future when those words would apply to her. How long had she been in love with him? It wasn't something she could pin an exact time or date to. She had always thought falling in love would be a light bulb moment, a flash of realisation that this was *The One*. But with Cam it had been more of a slow build, a gradual awareness the feelings she had towards him were no longer the platonic ones she had felt before. It was an awakening of her mind and body. Every moment she spent with him she loved him more. Which would make the end of their affair all the more difficult to deal with. Had she made a mistake in letting it go this far? But then she would never have known this magic. She would never have known the depth of pleasure her body was capable of giving and receiving.

The song ended and Cam led her back to their table in the corner to collect their coats. Violet suppressed a shiver when his hands pulled her hair out from the back of her collar when he helped her into her coat. She turned back around to face him and her belly did a flip at the smouldering look in his eyes. 'Time to go home?' she asked.

His mouth tilted in a sexy smile. 'If I make it that far.'

They barely made it through the door. Violet slipped out of her coat and walked into Cam's arms, his head coming down to connect his mouth with hers in a hungry kiss that made her whole body tingle. His tongue entered her mouth with a determined thrust that mimicked the intention of his body. She sent her tongue into combat with his, stroking and darting away in turn, ramping up the heat firing between them.

His hands went to the zipper at the back of her

dress, sending it down her back, his hand sliding beneath the sagging fabric to bring her closer to the hardened length of him. His mouth continued its passionate assault on her senses, his teeth taking playful nips of her lower lip, pulling it out and releasing it, salving it with his tongue and then doing it all over again.

Desire roared through Violet's body with a force that was almost frightening in its intensity. She clawed at his clothing like a woman possessed, popping buttons off his shirt but beyond caring. She had to feel his hot male skin under her hands. *Now.* She unzipped him and dragged down his underwear, taking him in one hand, massaging, stroking up and down until he was fighting for the control they'd lost as soon as they'd stepped through the door. She sank to her knees in front of him, ignoring his token protest and put her mouth to him.

He allowed her a few moments of torturing him but finally hauled her upright, pushing her back against the wall, ruthlessly stripping her dress from her, leaving her in nothing but her tights and knickers and heels. He cupped her mound, grinding the heel of his hand against her ache of longing, his mouth back on hers, hard, insistent, desperate.

Violet fed off his mouth, her hands grasping him

by the buttocks, holding him to the throb of her female flesh. 'Please…*please…*' She didn't care that she was begging. She needed him like she had never needed him before.

Cam pulled off her tights, taking her knickers with them. He left her hanging there while he sourced a condom, swiftly applying it and then coming back to her, entering her in one deep thrust that made her senses go wild. He set a furious pace, unlike anything he had done before. It was like a force had taken over his body, a force he couldn't control. The same force that was thundering through her body, making her gasp and whimper and arch her spine and roll her hips to get the friction where she needed it most.

He hooked one of her legs over his hip and caressed her with his fingers, triggering an earthquake in her body. It threw her into a tailspin, into a wild maelstrom of sensations that powered through her from head to toe. Even the hairs on her head felt like they were spinning at the roots.

Cam followed with his own release in three hard thrusts that brought a harsh cry out from between his lips.

Violet's legs were threatening to send her to a puddle of limbs on the floor at his feet. She grasped at the edges of his opened shirt, which she hadn't managed to get off his body in time. 'Wow, we should go dancing more often.'

He gave a soft laugh, his breathing not quite back to normal. 'We should.'

Violet pulled her clothes back on while he dealt with the condom and his own clothes. If anyone had told her she would have acted with such wanton abandon even a week ago, she would have been shocked. But with Cam everything felt…right. She had the confidence to express herself sexually with him because she knew he would never ask her to do something she wasn't comfortable with. He always put her pleasure ahead of his own. He worshipped her body instead of using it to satisfy himself.

'We'll have an opportunity to dance at my father's wedding on Saturday,' Cam said once they had gone upstairs to prepare for bed.

Violet stalled in the process of unzipping her dress. 'You're not really expecting me to go with you, are you?'

He was sitting on the end of the bed, reaching down to untie his shoelaces, but looked up with a partial frown. 'Of course I want you there. We can fly up to Drummond Brae that evening. The wedding's in the morning so we should make it plenty of time for Christmas.'

Violet sank her teeth into her lip. 'I don't know...'

'What's wrong?'

'Your father won't mind if I don't show up. He won't even notice.'

'Maybe not, but I want you there. I'm the best man. Dad's arranged to have you with me at the top table.'

Violet thought about the wedding photos that would be taken. How she would be in all the family shots that for years later everyone would look at and say, *'There's the girl who was engaged to Cam for two weeks.'* It was bad enough with it being all over social media. But at least everyone would forget about it after a while. But a wedding album wasn't the same as cyberspace. It would be a concrete reminder of a charade she should never have agreed to in the first place.

However, it wasn't just the fallout from social media that had her feeling so conflicted about his father's wedding. It was the wedding ceremony itself, the sanctity of it. How she felt she would be compromising someone else's special day by pretending to be something she was not. How could she cheapen a ceremony she held in such high esteem? It would be nothing short of sacrilege. 'I don't think I belong at your father's wedding.'

He got up from the bed and tossed his loosened

tie to the chest of drawers. 'You do belong there. You belong by my side as my fiancée.'

Violet pointedly raised her brow. 'Don't you mean your *fake* fiancée?'

A flicker of annoyance passed over his features. 'You didn't have any problem with lying to your workmates and your family. Why not stretch it to my family as well?'

'I'm not going, Cam. You can't make me.'

Cam came up to her and placed his hands on her shoulders. 'We're in this together, Violet. It's only till after Christmas. Surely it's not too much to ask you to come with me.'

Violet held his gaze. 'Why do you want me there? It's your father's fifth marriage, for pity's sake. It'll be a farcical version of what marriage is supposed to represent. I can't bear to be part of it. It would make me feel as if I'm poking fun at the institution I hold in the highest possible regard. Why is it so important to you that I be there?'

He dropped his hands and stepped away, his expression getting that boxed up look about it. 'Fine. Don't go. I don't blame you. I wish I didn't have to go either.'

Violet realised then how much he was dreading his father's wedding. Just like he had dreaded meeting his father for drinks. If she didn't go to the wedding then he would have to face it alone. Surely it was the least she could do to go with him and support him? He'd supported her at her office Christmas party. He'd supported her through the ordeal of her flat being broken in to. He'd been there for her every step of the way. It was a big compromise for her but wasn't that what all good relationships were about? She came up behind him and linked her arms around his waist. 'All right, I'll go with you but only because I care about you and hate the thought of you going through it alone.'

He turned and touched her gently on the cheek with his fingertip. 'I hate putting you through it. If it's anything like his last one it will be excruciating. But it'll be over by mid-afternoon and then we can fly up to Scotland to be with your family.'

Violet stepped up on tiptoe to plant a kiss to his lips. 'I can't wait.'

The church was full of flowers; every pew had a posy of blooms with a satin ribbon holding it in place. On each side of the altar was an enormous arrangement of red roses and another two at the back of the church. Violet sat in the pew and looked at Cam standing up at the altar with his father. Ross was joking and bantering with the other two groomsmen and, even though Violet was sitting a few rows back, she wondered if he was already a little drunk. His cheeks were ruddy and his movements were a little uncoordinated. Or perhaps it was wedding nerves? No. Ross McKinnon wasn't the type of man to get nervous about anything. He was enjoying being the centre of attention. He was relishing it. It was jarring for Violet, being such a romantic. She loved weddings where the groom looked nervous but excited waiting for his bride to arrive. Like her brother Fraser, who had kept checking his watch and swallowing deeply as the minutes ticked on. It had been such a beautiful wedding and Cam had been a brilliant best man.

Violet looked at Cam again. He looked composed. Too composed. Cardboard cut-out composed. He met her gaze and smiled. How she loved that smile. He only did it for her. It was *her* smile. The way his eyes lit up as if seeing her made him happy. She was glad she'd come to the wedding. It was the right thing to do even if the wedding was every type of wrong.

The organ started playing the 'Wedding March' and every head turned to the back of the church. There were three bridesmaids who were dressed in skimpy gowns that didn't suit their rather generous figures. Had Tatiana deliberately chosen friends who wouldn't upstage her? Not that anyone could upstage Tatiana. Violet heard the collective indrawn breath of the congregation when the bride appeared. Tatiana's white satin gown was slashed almost to the waist, with her cleavage on show as well as the slight bulge of her pregnancy. Violet looked on in horror as Tatiana's right breast threatened to pop out as she walked—strutted would be a more accurate description—up the aisle. The back of Tatiana's dress was similarly slashed, this time to the top of her buttocks, which her veil was not doing a particularly good job of hiding.

Ross looked like he couldn't wait to get his hands on his bride and made some joking aside to Cam that made Cam's jaw visibly tighten. Violet felt angry on his behalf. What a disgusting display of inappropriateness and poor Cam had to witness every second of it.

It got worse.

Ross and Tatiana had written the vows but they weren't romantic and heartfelt declarations but rather a travesty of what a marriage ceremony should be. Finally they were declared man and wife and Ross and Tatiana kissed for so long, with Ross's hand wandering all over his new bride's body, that several members of the congregation snickered.

The reception was little more than a drunken party. How Cam managed to get through his speech while his father cracked inappropriate jokes and drank copious amounts of champagne was anybody's guess.

When Cam sat back down beside her, she took his hand under the table and gave it a squeeze. 'This must be killing you,' she said.

'It'll be over soon.' He gave her a soft smile. 'How are you holding up?'

Violet curled her fingers around his. 'I'm fine, although I feel a bit silly up here at the top table. Tatiana doesn't like it. She keeps giving me the evil eye.'

'That's because you outshine her,' Cam said.

Violet could feel herself glowing at his compliment. His look warmed her blood. The look that said *I want you*. 'I'm going to powder my nose. Can we leave after that, do you think, or will we have to wait until your father and Tatiana leave?'

He glanced at his watch. 'Let's give it another hour and then we'll go.'

On her way back from the ladies' room, Violet saw Cam's father leading one of the bridesmaids by the hand to a corner behind a large arrangement of flowers. The bridesmaid was giggling and Ross was leering at her and groping her. Violet was so shocked she stood there with her mouth hanging open. Did Ross have no shame? He'd only been married a matter of hours and he was already straying. Did the commitment of marriage mean nothing to him?

Violet swung away and went back to where Cam was waiting for her. She couldn't stay another minute at this wretched farce of a wedding. Not. One. Minute. She felt tainted by it. Sullied. Defiled by listening to people mouthing words they didn't mean and watching them behaving like out of control teenagers. No wonder Cam was so against marriage. Apart from her brother and sisters' weddings, all he had seen was the repeated drunken mockery of what was supposed to be the most important day in a couple's life. No wonder he was cynical. No wonder he couldn't picture himself getting married in the near future.

'What's wrong?' Cam said when she snatched up her wrap from the back of the chair.

'I can't stay here another minute,' Violet said. 'Your father is feeling up one of the bridesmaids out in the foyer.'

Cam's expression showed little surprise about his father's behaviour. 'Yes, well, that's my father for you. A class act at all times and in all places.'

Violet tugged his arm. 'Come on. Let's get out of here. My flesh is crawling. Oh, God, look at Tatiana. She's got her tongue in the groomsman's ear. She's practically doing a lap dance on him.'

Cam took Violet's hand and led her out of the reception room. 'Sorry you had to witness all that craziness. But I'm glad you came. It would've been unbearable without you there.'

Violet was still seething about his father's and Tatiana's behaviour when they got home to change and collect their bags for their evening flight to Scotland. 'I can't believe you share any of your father's DNA. You're nothing like him. You're decent and caring and principled. I'm sure if you were to get married one day in the future you won't be off canoodling with one of the bridesmaids within an hour or two of the ceremony. What is wrong with him?'

Cam paused in the action of slipping off his coat. But then he resumed the process of shrugging it off and hanging it on the hallstand with what seemed to Violet somewhat exaggerated precision. 'We've had this conversation a number of times before,' he said. 'I don't want to get married.'

Violet felt his words like a rusty stake to her heart. Not married? *Ever?* She had heard him say it before but hadn't things been changing between them? Hadn't *she* changed things for him? He cared about her. He talked to her. *Really* talked. About things he'd not spoken of to anyone else. He had invited her into his home. Was his heart really still so off-limits? How could he make love to her the way he had and not have felt anything? He'd bought her an engagement ring, for goodness' sake. He could have bought something cheap but he'd chosen something so special, so perfect, it surely meant he cared more than he wanted to admit.

Violet understood now why he was so wary of marriage. But deep down she had harboured hope that he would see how a marriage between them would be just like the marriage between her parents: respectful and loving and lasting. 'You don't really mean that, Cam. Deep down you want what I want. What my parents and siblings have. You've seen how a good marriage is conducted. You can't let your father's atrocious behaviour influence you like this. You're not living his life, you're living yours.'

Cam's expression went into lockdown. Violet knew him well enough to know he felt cornered. A frown formed between his eyes, his mouth tightened and a muscle ticked in his lean cheek. 'Violet.'

'Don't *do* that,' Violet said, frustrated beyond measure. 'Don't use that schoolmaster tone with me as if I'm too stupid to know what I'm talking about. You're not facing what's right in front of you. I know you care about me. You care about me much more than you want to admit. I can't go on pretending to be engaged to you when all I want is for it to be for real.'

The tenseness around his mouth travelled all the way up to his eyes. They were hard as flint. 'Then you'll be waiting a long time because I'm not going to change my mind.'

Violet knew it was time for a line to be drawn. How long could she go on hoping he would come to see things her way? What if she stayed in a relationship with him for months and months, maybe even years, and he still wouldn't budge? All her dreams of a beautiful wedding day with her whole family there would be destroyed. All her hopes for a family of her own would be shattered. She couldn't give that up. She loved him. She loved him desperately but she wouldn't be true to herself if she drifted along in a going nowhere relationship with him. She had to make a stand. She couldn't go on living in this excruciating limbo of will-he-or-won't-he? She had to make him see there was no future without a proper commitment.

No fling.

No temporary arrangement.

No pretend engagement.

Violet drew in a carefully measured breath, garnering her resolve. 'Then I don't want you to come home to Drummond Brae with me. I'd rather go alone.'

It was hard to tell if her statement affected him for hardly a muscle moved on his face. 'Fine.'

Fine? Violet's heart gave a painful spasm. How could he be so calm and clinical about this? Didn't he feel anything for her? Maybe he didn't love her after all. Maybe all this had been a convenient affair that had a use-by date. *Be strong. Be strong. Be strong.* She knew he was expecting her to cave in. It was what she did all the time. She over-adapted. She compromised. She hated hurting people's feelings so she ended up saying yes when she meant no. It had to stop. It had to stop now. It was time to grow a backbone. 'Is that your final decision?' she said.

'Violet, you're being unreasonable about—'

'*I'm* being unreasonable?' Violet said. 'What's unreasonable about wanting to be happy? I can't be happy with you if you're not one hundred per cent committed to me. I can't live like that. I don't want to miss out on all the things I've dreamt about since I was a little girl. If you don't want the same things then it's time to call it quits before we end up hurting each other too much.'

'It was never my intention to hurt you,' Cam said.

You just did. 'I have to go now or I'll miss the flight.' Violet moved past him to collect her bag from his room upstairs. Would he follow her and try and talk her out of it? Would he tell her how much he loved her? She listened for the sound of his tread on the stairs but there was nothing but silence.

When she came back downstairs with her overnight bag he was still standing in the hall with that blank expression. 'I'll drive you to the airport,' he said, barely moving his lips as he spoke.

'That won't be necessary,' Violet said. 'I've already called a cab.' She took off her engagement ring and handed it to him. 'I won't be needing this any more.'

He ignored her outstretched hand. 'Keep it.'

'I don't want to keep it.'

'Sell it and give the money to charity.'

Violet placed the ring on the table next to his keys. Did it have to end like this? With them acting like stiff strangers at the end of the affair? She'd taken a gamble and it hadn't paid off. It was supposed to pay off! Why wasn't he putting his hands on her shoulders and turning her around and smiling at her with that tender smile he reserved only for her? She turned back to face him but if he were feeling even half of the heartache she was, he showed no sign of it. 'Goodbye, Cam. I guess I'll see you when I see you.'

'I guess you will.'

Violet put on her gloves and rewound her scarf around her neck. *Do* not *cry.*

'Right, that's it then. I'll have to collect the rest of my things when I get back. I hope it's okay to leave them here until then?'

'Of course it is.'

Another silence passed.

Violet heard the telltale beep of the taxi outside. Cam took her bag for her and opened the front door and helped her into the taxi. He couldn't have given her a clearer message that he was 'fine' with her decision to leave without him.

Violet slipped into the back of the taxi without kissing him goodbye. There was only so much heartbreak she could cope with. Touching him one last time would be her undoing. She didn't want to turn into a mess to add insult to injury. If it was over then it was over. Better to be quick and clean about it. Apparently he felt the same way because he simply closed the door of the taxi and stood back from the kerb as if he couldn't wait for it to take her away.

'Going home for Christmas?' the cabbie asked.

Violet swallowed as Cam's statue-like figure gradually disappeared from view. 'Yes,' she said on a sigh. 'I'm going home.'

CHAPTER NINE

CAM STOOD WATCHING the taxi until it disappeared around the corner. *What are you doing?* Being sensible, that was what he was doing. If he chased after her and begged her to stay then what would it achieve? A few weeks, a few months of a relationship that was the best he'd ever had but could go no further. That was what he would have.

He walked back into his house and picked up the engagement ring off the table. It was still warm from being on Violet's finger. Why was he feeling so...numb? Like the world had dropped out from under him.

Violet had blindsided him with her ultimatum. He was already feeling raw from his father's ridiculous sham of a wedding. She couldn't have picked a worse time to discuss the future of their relationship. Seeing his father act like a horny teenager all through that farce of a service, and then to hear via

Violet he had been feeling up one of the bridesmaids at the reception had made Cam deeply ashamed. So ashamed he'd wanted to distance himself from anything to do with weddings. The word was enough to make him want to be ill. Why had she done that? Why push him when they'd already discussed it? He had been honest and upfront about it. He hadn't told her any lies, made any false commitments, allowed her to believe there was a pot of gold at the end of the rainbow. They hadn't been together long enough to be talking of marriage even if he was the marrying type. If he were going to propose for real—*if*—then he would do it in his own good time, not because it was demanded of him.

Go after her.

Cam took one step towards the door but then stopped. Of course he had to let her go. What was the point in dragging this out till after Christmas? It wasn't fair to her and it wasn't fair to her family. She wanted more than he was prepared to give. She wanted the fairytale. Damn it, she *deserved* the fairytale. All her life she had been waiting for Mr Right and Cam was only getting in the way of her finding him.

He paced the floor, torn between wanting to chase after her and staying put where his life was under his control. He blew out a long breath and went through to the sitting room. He sat on one of the sofas and cradled his head in his hands. His chest felt like someone had dragged his heart from his body, leaving a gaping hole.

If this was the right thing to do then why did it feel so goddamn painful?

Violet hadn't worked up the courage to tell her parents she and Cam were finished when her mother texted to ask what time they would be arriving. She told her mother they would be arriving separately due to his father's wedding commitments. She knew it was cowardly but she couldn't cope with their disappointment when hers was still so raw and painful. Checking into that flight at Heathrow had been one of the loneliest moments of her life. Even as she'd boarded the plane, she had hoped Cam would come rushing up behind her and spin her around to face him, saying he had made the biggest mistake of his life to let her leave.

But he hadn't turned up. He hadn't even texted or phoned. Didn't that prove how relieved he was that their relationship was over? By delivering an ultimatum she had given him a get-out-of-jail-free card. No wonder he hadn't argued the point or asked for more time on their relationship. He had grabbed the opportunity to end it.

Violet's mother met her at the airport and swept her into a bone-crushing hug. 'Poppet! I'm so happy to see you. Your father's at home making mince pies. Yes, mince pies! Isn't he a sweetheart trying to help? But you should see the mess he's making in the kitchen. We'll be cleaning up flour for weeks. Now, what time is Cam coming? There are only two more flights this evening. I've already checked. I hope he doesn't miss whichever one he's on. I've made up the suite in the east wing for you both. It's like a honeymoon suite.'

Violet let her mother's cheerful chatter wash over her. It reminded her of the time when she'd come home after quitting university. She had kept her pain and shame hidden rather than burst her mother's bubble of happiness at having her youngest child back home. It wasn't that her mother wasn't sensitive, but rather Violet was adept at concealing her emotions.

Her father was at the front door of Drummond Brae wearing a flour-covered apron when Violet and her mother arrived. He came rushing down the steps and gathered her in a hug that made her feet come off the ground. 'Welcome home, wee one,' he said. 'Come away inside out of the cold. It's going to snow for Christmas. We've already had a flurry or two.'

Violet stepped over the threshold and came face to face with a colourful banner hanging across the foyer that said: *Congratulations Cam and Violet*. Helium balloons with her and Cam's names on them danced in the draught of cold air from the open door, their tinsel strings hanging like silver tails.

Her grandfather came shuffling in on his walking frame, his wrinkled face beaming from ear to ear. 'Let's see that ring of yours, little Vivi,' he said.

Violet swallowed a knot that felt as big as a pine cone off the Christmas tree towering in the hall in all its festive glory. She kept her gloves on, too embarrassed to show her empty ring finger. How on earth was she going to tell them? The rest of the family came bursting in, Fraser and Zoe with their twins Ben and Mia and then Rose and Alex with their boys Jack and Jonathon. And, of course, Gertie the elderly golden retriever who looked like the canine version of Grandad with her creaky gait and whitened snout.

'Aunty Violet! Did you bring me a present?' Ben asked with a cheeky grin, so like her brother Fraser it made Violet's heart contract.

'Can I be your flower girl?' Mia asked, hugging Violet around the waist.

Rose and Lily greeted her with big smiles and even bigger hugs. 'We've already started on the champagne,' Rose said. 'Well, not Lily, of course, but I'm drinking her share.'

'When's Cam arriving?' Lily asked.

'Erm…' Violet felt tears burning like acid behind her eyes. 'He's…hoping to make it in time for Christmas dinner.' *Coward.*

Her brother Fraser came forward and gave her a big hug. 'So pleased for you guys. Always knew Cam had a thing for you.'

'I thought so too,' Rose said, grinning. 'He wasn't himself at Easter, do you remember, Lil? Remember when I asked him to take in a hot cross bun to Vivi and he got all flustered and said he had to make a call? Classic. Absolutely classic.'

Lily's smile made her eyes dance. 'I'm so thrilled for you, Vivi. All three of us will be married. How soon will you start a family? It'd be so cool to have our kids close in age.'

Gertie came up to Violet and slowly wagged her tail and gave a soft whine as if to say, *What's wrong?*

Violet could stand it no longer. 'I—I have something to tell you…'

Rose's eyes lit up as bright as the lights on the

Christmas tree she was standing near. 'You're pregnant?'

Violet bit her lip so hard she thought she would break the skin. 'Cam and I are...not engaged.'

The stunned silence was so profound no one moved. Not even the children. Even the tinsel and baubles on the Christmas tree seemed to be holding themselves stock-still. Everyone was looking at her as if she had just told them she had a disease and it was contagious.

'Oh, poppet.' Her mother came to her and gathered her in her arms, rocking her from side to side as if she were still a baby. 'I'm so sorry.'

Her father joined in the hug, gently patting her on the back with soothing 'there, there's' that made Violet sob all the harder.

Rose and Lily ushered the children away and Fraser helped Grandad back into the sitting room near the fire. Lily's husband Cooper and Rose's husband Alex came in late and, taking one look at the scene, promptly walked back out.

'What happened?' Violet's mother asked. 'Did he break it off?'

'No, I did. But we weren't even engaged. We were pretending.'

Her mother frowned. 'Pretending?'

Violet explained the situation through a series

of hiccupping sobs. 'It's my fault for being so pathetic about going to the office Christmas party on my own. I should've just gone alone and not been such a stupid baby. Now I've hurt everyone and ruined my friendship with Cam and spoilt Christmas for everyone too.'

'You haven't spoilt anything, poppet,' her mother said. 'Take the banner down, Gavin. And get the kids to pop the balloons. I'll take Violet upstairs.'

Violet followed her mother upstairs, not to the suite prepared for her and Cam but to her old bedroom. All her childhood toys were neatly arranged on top of the dresser and some on her bed. Violet's books were in the bookshelves, waiting for her like old friends. It was like stepping back in time but feeling out of place. She wasn't a child any more. She was an adult with adult needs. Needs Cam had awakened and then walked away from as if they meant nothing to him.

As if *she* meant nothing to him.

Her mother sat on the edge of the bed beside Violet. 'Are you in love with him?'

'Yes, but he doesn't love me. Well, he does but not like that.'

'Did you tell him you loved him?'

Violet gave a despondent sigh. 'What would be

the point? He never wants to get married. He doesn't want kids either.'

'I expect that's because of his parents,' her mother said. 'But he might change his mind.'

'He won't.'

Her mother hugged her again. 'My poor baby. I wish there was something I could do or say to help you feel better.'

Violet wiped at her eyes with her sleeve. 'I love him so much but he's so cynical about getting married. Deep down, I don't really blame him after attending his father's fifth wedding today. It was awful. So awful you wouldn't believe.' She described some of what went on and her mother made tut-tutting noises and shook her head in disgust.

'Did you press him for a commitment after you came back from the wedding?' her mother asked.

Violet looked at her mum's frowning expression. 'You think I should've waited?'

Her mother squeezed her hand. 'What's done is done. At least you were honest with him. No point pretending you're happy when you're not.'

Violet's bottom lip quivered. 'He's the only one for me, Mum. I know I won't be happy with anyone else. I just know it.'

Her mother gave her a sad smile. 'For your sake, poppet, I hope that's not true.'

* * *

Cam packed up Violet's things for when she was ready to collect them. He could have done it any time between Christmas and New Year because she wouldn't be back till the second of January as they had planned to spend the week with her family. But he was feeling restless and on edge. He kept telling himself it was better this way. That it was wrong to drag things out when he couldn't give her what she wanted.

But when he came to her embroidery basket, his heart gave a painful spasm. He opened the lid and took out the creamy baby blanket Violet was in the process of embroidering with tiny flowers. He held it to his face, its softness reminding him of her skin. He could even smell her on the blanket—that sweet flowery scent that made him think of spring. He put the blanket back inside the basket and took out a pair of booties. They were so tiny he couldn't imagine a baby's foot small enough to fit them. He started to picture a baby…one he and Violet might make together: a little squirming body with dimpled hands and feet, a downy dark head with eyes bright and clear and a little rosebud mouth.

What if Violet were pregnant? They had been careful but accidents could happen. Should he call her? No. Too soon. He needed more time. Time to get his head together. He wasn't used to feeling this level of emotion. This sense of…loss. The sense of loss was so acute it felt like a giant hole, leaving him empty and raw.

Cam picked up a tiny jacket that had sailing boats embroidered around the collar. He rubbed his thumb over the meticulous stitches, wondering what it would be like to have a son. His father hadn't been an active father in any sense of the word, but Cam couldn't imagine not wanting to be involved in your child's life. How could you not be interested in your own flesh and blood? Being there for every milestone, watching them grow and develop, reading to them at bedtime—all the things Violet's parents had done and were now doing for each of their grandchildren when they came to stay.

He put the sailing boat jacket down and picked up a pink cardigan that was so small it would have looked at home on a doll. There were tiny rosebuds around the collar and the cuffs of the sleeves. What would it be like to have a daughter? To watch her grow from babyhood to womanhood. To be there for her first smile, her first tooth, her first steps. *Gulp*. Her first date. Walking her down the aisle. One day becoming a grandfather…

Cam had never thought about having his own children. Well, he had thought about it but just as quickly dismissed it. Like when he had walked into the sitting room at Drummond Brae at Easter and seen Violet curled up on the sofa with a baby's bonnet in her hands. It had been a jarring reminder of the responsibility he'd spent his adult life actively avoiding.

But now he wondered why he was working so hard when he had no one to share it with. What was the point? Would he end up some lonely old man living out his end days alone? Not surrounded by a loving family like Grandad Archie in the winter of his life. No one to tell him they loved him, no one to be there in sickness and in health and everything in between. No laughter-filled Christmases with all the family gathered around the tree exchanging gifts and smiles and love.

Cam put the pink cardigan back inside the basket and closed the lid. What was he doing? It was best this way. Violet was better off without him and his crazy family who would do nothing but stir up trouble between them if given half a chance. He wasn't cut out for marriage and commitment. He was too driven by his career, by achieving, by the next task waiting on his desk. He didn't have the time to invest in a long-term relationship.

Cam had been to three of his father's previous weddings and never once taken much notice of the vows. But when he'd heard his father make all those promises earlier that day it had made Cam's gut churn to realise his father didn't mean a word of them. They were just words, empty, meaningless words because his father had no intention of committing to his new wife other than in an outward way by standing up in church in front of family and friends. His father didn't mean them on the inside, in his heart where it counted. Anyone could say they would love someone for the rest of their life but how many people actually meant it? Violet's parents obviously had. So had her grandad Archie and Maisie Drummond when they had married sixty-five years ago.

Cam knew if it were him up there saying those words with Violet by his side, he would make sure he meant them. His heart gave a kick as the realisation dawned. This was why he had avoided marriage and commitment all this time—because he had never been able to picture himself saying those words with any sincerity. But with Violet they meant everything. He loved her with all his heart and mind and soul. He worshipped her with his body, he wanted to protect her and stand by her in sickness and in health, in pregnancy and childbirth.

What a damn fool he had been. Letting her walk

away when he loved her so much. Loved her more than anything, more than his freedom, which wasn't such a great thing anyway. True freedom was in your ability to love someone without fear, without conditions, loving without restraint.

The love he felt for Violet was bigger than his fear of abandonment. It was bigger than the need to protect himself from hurt. He couldn't control life and all its vagaries. Life happened, no matter how carefully you laid plans. He thought of Violet's poor workmate Kenneth, so hung up on his ex-wife he was unable to move on with his life. Cam didn't want to be like that. Too afraid to love in case he lost it.

He loved Violet and he would make sure nothing and no one destroyed that love. They would face the future together, a dedicated team who had each other's backs no matter what.

Cam glanced at his watch. He would have to hotfoot it but he could make the last flight if he was lucky.

Violet was determined her family's Christmas would not suffer any more disturbance after her tearful confession. She joined in with the family board games—a Drummond tradition late at night on Christmas Eve while everyone drank eggnog— and laughed at her father's corny jokes and patiently repeated everything for Grandad, who was hard of hearing. Her mother kept a watchful eye on her, but Violet did her best to assure her mum she was doing just fine, even though on the inside she felt a cavern of emptiness.

She couldn't stop wondering what Cam was doing. Was he spending Christmas with his mother or alone? Or had he hooked up with someone new? It wasn't like him to do something like that but what if he wanted to press home a point? He wanted his freedom, otherwise wouldn't he have come after her by now? Called her? Texted her? Given her a fragment of hope? No. He hadn't. It didn't seem fair that she was up here in the Highlands of Scotland nursing a broken heart while he was in London living the life of a playboy. Did he miss her? Was he thinking about her?

'Well, we're off to bed,' Fraser announced, taking Zoe's hand. 'The kids will be up at four, looking for their presents.'

Zoe gave Violet a sad look. 'Are you okay, Vivi?'

Violet put on a brave smile. 'Rose and I are going to work on that bottle of champagne over there, aren't we, Rose?'

Rose gave her an apologetic look and reached for her husband Alex's hand. 'Sorry, Vivi, but I've had too much already.'

'Don't look at me,' Lily said, placing a protective hand over her belly. 'I'm knackered in any case.'

'Will you take Gertie out for a wee walk, poppet?' her mother asked. 'Your father and I have to stuff the turkey.'

Violet shrugged on her coat and put on her gloves and took the dog outside into the crisp night air. There were light flurries of snow but it wasn't settling. So much for a magical white Christmas. Maybe it was going to be one of those miserable grey and gloomy ones, which would be rather fitting for her current state of mind.

Gertie wasn't content with waddling about the garden and instead put her nose down to follow a scent leading down to the loch. Violet grabbed a torch from the hall table drawer and followed the dog. The loch was a silver shape in the moonlight, the forest behind it a dense dark fringe.

Violet stood at the water's edge, feeling the biting cold coming off the sheet of water while Gertie bustled about in the shadows. An owl hooted, a vixen called out for a mate.

A twig snapped under someone's foot.

Violet spun around, shining the torch in the direction of the sound. 'Who's there?'

Cam stepped into the beam of light. 'It's me.'

Violet's heart gave an almighty lurch. 'Cam?'

He shielded his eyes with his arm. 'Will you stop shining that thing in my face?'

'Sorry.' She lowered the torch. 'You scared the heck out of me.'

He came up closer, the moonlight casting his features into ghostly relief. Gertie padded over and gave him an enthusiastic greeting as if she had suddenly turned into a puppy instead of the fifteen-year-old dog she was. Cam leaned down to scratch at the dog's ears before straightening. 'I'm sorry about earlier today. I was wrong to let you leave like that. I got flooded with feelings I didn't want to acknowledge. But I'm acknowledging them now. I love you, Violet. I love you and want to spend the rest of my life with you. Will you marry me?'

Violet stared at him, wondering if she was hearing things. 'Did you just ask me to marry you?'

He smiled so tenderly it made her heart skip a beat. Her smile. The one he only used for her. 'I did and I want to have babies with you. We can be a family like your family. We can do it because we're a team who are batting for each other, not against each other.'

Violet stepped into his waiting arms, nestling her head against his chest. 'I love you so much. It tore my heart out to leave you but I had to. I wasn't being true to myself or to you. Your father's wedding brought it home to me. I couldn't go on pretending.'

'After you left I started thinking about my father and that ridiculous sham of a wedding,' Cam said. 'He doesn't love Tatiana enough to die for her. He's using her as a trophy to prove his diminishing potency. He uses every woman he's ever been with like that. I know I won't do that to you. I couldn't. You mean the world to me. I couldn't possibly love anyone more than I love you.'

Violet gazed up at him. Was this really happening? Cam was here. In person. Asking her to marry him. Telling her he loved her more than anyone else in the world. 'It was a bit mean of me to push you on commitment so close to your father's wedding,' she said. 'No wonder you backed away. The mere mention of the word *wedding* after that debacle of a ceremony would've been enough to make you run for cover.'

He gave her a rueful smile. 'Your timing was a little off but I got there eventually. I'm sorry you had to go through an awful few hours thinking we were over. After you left I sat in numb shock. Nor-

mally when a relationship of mine comes to an end
I feel relieved. Not this time. Can you forgive me
for being so blockheaded?'

Violet linked her arms around his neck. 'I'm
never leaving again. Not ever. You've made all my
dreams come true. You've even proposed to me by
the loch.'

He grinned and drew her closer. 'I reckon we've
got about sixty seconds before your family come
down here to check if there's a reason to celebrate
Christmas with a bang or we both freeze to death.
Will you marry me, my darling?'

Violet smiled so widely her face ached. 'Yes. A
million times yes.'

'Once will be more than enough,' Cam said.
'From here on I'm a one-woman man.'

She stroked his lean jaw, now dark and rough
with stubble. 'I've been a one-man woman for a
lot longer. I think that's probably why I never dated
with any enthusiasm. I was subconsciously waiting for you.'

His eyes became shadowed for a moment as if he
was recalling how close to losing her he had come.
'How could I have been so stupid not to see how
perfect you are for me all this time?'

Violet smiled. 'Mum saw it. She's going to be beside herself when she hears you're here. Did anyone see you coming up the driveway?'

'I'm not sure. When I pulled up I caught a glimpse of you heading towards the lake with Gertie so I came straight down here.'

'They made a banner for us,' Violet said. 'It was a bad moment when I saw it hanging in the hall. I hadn't told them we were over at that point.'

He winced. 'Poor you. Well, we'd better tell them the good news. Ready?'

Violet drew his head down to hers. 'Not yet. Let's treasure this moment for our kids. I want to tell them how you kissed me in the moonlight, just like Grandad did to my grandmother in exactly this spot.'

'Hang on, I'm forgetting something.' He took out the ring from his pocket and slipped it on her finger. 'I don't want to see that come off again.'

Violet smiled as she twirled the ring on her finger. Her hand had felt so strange without it there. Like someone else's hand. The diamond winked at her as if to say, *I'm back!* 'I can't believe this is happening. I felt so lonely and lost without you.'

'Me too,' he said. 'I was so afraid of losing you that I ended up losing you. I will regret to the day I die not following you out of my house and bringing you back. I wanted to but I kept thinking you were better off without me.'

There was the sound of twigs snapping and a few hushed whispers. Cam's eyes twinkled. 'Looks like the family has arrived. Shall we make an announcement?'

Violet drew his head down to hers. 'Let's show them instead.'

EPILOGUE

Christmas Eve the following year...

CAM LOOKED AROUND the sitting room at Drummond Brae where all Violet's family were gathered. Correction. *His* and Violet's family. The last few months since his and Violet's wedding in June had shown him more than ever how important family was and how much he had missed out on having a proper one growing up. But he was more than making up for it now. He glanced at Violet where she was sitting almost bursting to tell the family her good news. *Their* good news. He still couldn't believe they were having a baby. Violet was just past the twelve-week mark and there could be no better Christmas present for her parents than to tell them they were about to have another grandchild.

He smiled when Violet's gaze met his. He never tired of looking at her; she was glowing but not just because of being pregnant. She had completed her first semester of an English Literature degree. He couldn't have been prouder of her. Of course she topped her class.

Grandad Archie was sitting with a blanket over his legs and a glass of whisky in his hand and looking at Violet with a smile on his face. That was another miracle Cam felt grateful for. Grandad Archie, while certainly not robust in health, was at least enjoying life surrounded by his beloved family. Even Kenneth, Violet's workmate, had started dating again. Cam had introduced him to a young widow who worked part-time in his office and they'd hit it off and had been seeing each other ever since.

Poor old Gertie, the golden retriever, hadn't been so lucky; her ashes were spread out by the loch not far from where Cam had proposed to Violet. But there was a new addition to the family, a ten-week-old puppy called Nessie who was currently chewing on one of Cam's shoelaces.

'Vivi, why aren't you drinking your eggnog?' Grandad Archie asked with a twinkle in his eyes. 'Is there something you have to tell us?'

Cam took Violet's hand just as she reached for his. He squeezed it gently, his heart so full of love he could feel his chest swelling like bread dough.

'We have an announcement to make,' he said. 'We're having a baby.'

'Ach, now I'll have to live another year so I can wet the wee one's head,' Grandad said, grinning from ear to ear.

Violet's mother grasped her husband's hand and blinked back happy tears. 'We're so thrilled for you both. It's just the most wonderful news.'

Violet placed Cam's hand on the tiny swell of her belly and smiled up at him with her beautiful brown eyes brimming with happiness. 'I love you.'

Cam bent down and kissed her tenderly. 'I love you too. Happy Christmas, my darling.'

'Okay, knock it off you two,' Fraser said with a cheeky grin. 'The honeymoon's been over for six months.'

Cam grinned back. 'Not this honeymoon.' He gathered Violet closer. 'This one's going to last for ever.'

* * * * *

#3485 THE PRINCE'S PREGNANT MISTRESS

Heirs Before Vows

by Maisey Yates

"I'm pregnant." It takes two words to see Prince Raphael DeSantis bound to a *waitress*. Now to prevent an international incident, Raphael must marry his mistress! But heartsore Bailey won't come willingly. Raphael must seduce Bailey Harper into submission...

#3486 THE GUARDIAN'S VIRGIN WARD

One Night With Consequences

by Caitlin Crews

Domineering Spaniard Izar Agustin couldn't have imagined that his ward, innocent Liliana Girard Brooks, would become such an alluring woman. One night of sensual abandon shows Liliana the unconscious desires of her body... But the consequences of that night bind them together...forever!

#3487 THE DESERT KING'S SECRET HEIR

Secret Heirs of Billionaires

by Annie West

Surrounded by society's glitterati, Arden Wills is confronted with her first and only love, Idris Baddour—a man she never knew was a sheikh! When their ardent kiss is blasted across the world's media, Arden's secret comes to light—the Sheikh has a son!

#3488 SURRENDERING TO THE VENGEFUL ITALIAN

Irresistible Mediterranean Tycoons

by Angela Bissell

Not even his foe's stunning daughter, Helena Shaw, will halt Leonardo Vincenti's vengeance. Leo knows that Helena would never willingly return to his side, so he blackmails her. But the passion that undid them before soon forces them *both* to the brink of surrender...

YOU CAN FIND MORE INFORMATION ON UPCOMING HARLEQUIN° TITLES, FREE EXCERPTS AND MORE AT WWW.HARLEQUIN.COM.

HPCNM1116RB

SPECIAL EXCERPT FROM

HARLEQUIN *Presents*

*Natalia Di Sione hasn't left the family estate in years,
but she must retrieve her grandfather's lost book of
poems from Angelos Menas! The lives of the brooding
Greek and his daughter were changed irrevocably by
a fire, and Talia finds herself drawn to the formidable
tycoon. She knows the untold pleasure Angelos offers
is limited, but when she leaves with the book, will her
heart remain on the island?*

Read on for a sneak preview of
A DI SIONE FOR THE GREEK'S PLEASURE,
the sixth in the unmissable new eight book
Harlequin Presents® series
THE BILLIONAIRE'S LEGACY.

"Talia..." Angelos's voice broke on her name, and then,
before she could even process what was happening, he
pulled her toward him, his hands hard on her shoulders as his
mouth crashed down on hers and plundered its soft depths.

It had been ten years since she'd been kissed, and then
only a schoolboy's buss. She'd never been kissed like this,
never felt every sense blaze to life, every nerve ending tingle
with awareness, nearly painful in its intensity, as Angelos's
mouth moved on hers and he pulled her tightly to him.

His hard contours collided against her softness, each
point of contact creating an unbearably exquisite ache of
longing as she tangled her hands in his hair and fit her mouth
against his.

She was a clumsy, inexpert kisser, not sure what to do
with her lips or tongue, only knowing that she wanted more
of this. Of him.

She felt his hand slide down to cup her breast, his palm hot and hard through the thin material of her dress, and a gasp of surprise and delight escaped her.

That small sound of pleasure was enough to jolt Angelos out of his passion-fogged daze, for he dropped his hand and in one awful, abrupt movement tore his mouth from hers and stepped back.

"I'm sorry," he said, his voice coming out in a ragged gasp.

"No…" Talia pressed one shaky hand to her buzzing lips as she tried to blink the world back into focus. "Don't be sorry," she whispered. "It was wonderful."

"I shouldn't have—"

"Why not?" she challenged. She felt frantic with the desperate need to feel and taste him again, and more important, not to have him withdraw from her, not just physically, but emotionally. Angelos didn't answer and she forced herself to ask the question again. "Why not, Angelos?"

"Because you are my employee, and I was taking advantage of you," he gritted out. "It was not appropriate…"

"I don't care about appropriate," she cried. She knew she sounded desperate and even pathetic but she didn't care. She wanted him. She needed him. "I care about you," she confessed, her voice dropping to a choked whisper, and surprise and something worse flashed across Angelos's face. He shook his head, the movement almost violent and terribly final.

"No, Talia," he told her flatly. "You don't."

Don't miss
A DI SIONE FOR THE GREEK'S PLEASURE,
available December 2016 wherever
Harlequin Presents® books and ebooks are sold.

www.Harlequin.com